Mates, Dates & Pulling Power

Cathy Hopkins is the author of the incredibly successful *Mates, Dates* and *Truth, Dare* books, and has started a fabulous new series called *Cinnamon Girl.* She lives in North London with her husband and three cats, Molly, Emmylou and Otis.

Cathy spends most of her time locked in a shed at the bottom of the garden pretending to write books but is actually in there listening to music, hippie dancing and talking to her friends on e-mail.

Occasionally she is joined by Molly, the cat who thinks she is a copy-editor and likes to walk all over the keyboard rewriting and deleting any words she doesn't like.

Emmylou and Otis are new to the household. So far they are as insane as the older one. Their favourite game is to run from one side of the house to the other as fast as possible, then see if they can fly if they leap high enough off the furniture. This usually happens at three o'clock in the morning and they land on anyone who happens to be asleep at the time.

Apart from that, Cathy has joined the gym and spends more time than is good for her making up excuses as to why she hasn't got time to go.

Cathy Hopkins

Mates, Dates & Pulling Power

PICCADILLY PRESS • LONDON

Thanks as always to Brenda Gardner, Yasemin Uçar and the ever fab team at Piccadilly Press. To Rosemary Bromley at Juvenelia. To Steve Lovering for all his help and support. To Peter Ziderman for his input about dentists and braces. And to Georgina Acar, Scott and Jack Brenman, Alice Elwes, Rachel Hopkins and Olivia McDonnell for answering all my questions about what it's like being a teenager these days.

First published in Great Britain in 2003
by Piccadilly Press Ltd.,
5 Castle Road, London NW1 8PR

This edition published 2007

A catalogue record for this book is available from the British Library

ISBN: 978 1 85340 933 2 (trade paperback)

1 3 5 7 9 10 8 6 4 2

Printed in the UK by CPI Bookmarque, Croydon, CR0 4TD
Typeset by Textype Typesetters
Cover design by Simon Davis

Set in 11.5pt Bembo and Lush

Chapter 1

Ghastly Ghoul Face Packs

'Pah,' I said. 'I wouldn't go out with Adrian Cook if he was dipped in gold and covered in fivers.'

Izzie gave me a disapproving look. '*Nesta*. Covered in fivers? You mean, if he was loaded. So what? I don't think how rich or poor a boy is should make the slightest bit of difference. It's who he is, if he's interesting, good company that counts.'

I pulled a silly face back at her. She can be a real priss queen sometimes. 'Yeah, but he has to be *reasonably* cute,' I said.

'So what if he's cute,' asked Izzie, 'if he's boring to be with? Just good looks don't count for much after a few dates. You always judge by externals.'

'Do not.'

'Do.'

'Not.'

The four of us were sitting in a line on the edge of the bathtub in the bathroom at Lucy's house. TJ, Izzie, Lucy and me. We were covered in some homemade facial gloop that Lucy and Izzie had concocted in the kitchen and were discussing the local boy talent in North London. Pretty short on the ground in my opinion. And I *don't* only judge by externals, I thought. Of course I care what a boy's like inside.

'Beauty is only skin deep,' said TJ, peering at herself in the mirror opposite.

'Yeah, but not today,' I replied, looking at our reflections. 'We look like ghastly ghouls. What is in this stuff, Lucy? It feels very sticky. Are you sure you were meant to put so much honey in it?'

Lucy reached for her natural beauty book, which was on the windowsill. 'I think so,' she said. 'Yeah, egg yolk, yeast and honey.'

'Sounds disgusting,' I said. 'I wish you hadn't told me.'

It was Sunday and sometimes there's not a lot to do on a Sunday, especially if it's raining like it was today. Lucy suggested we have an afternoon of beauty treatments round at her house and as none of us were that well off in the pocket money department, she decided to make DIY face masks. Think I'll stick to nicking Mum's posh ones when she's out from now on,

I thought. Egg on my face? Never a good idea at the best of times.

'Well, if it doesn't work, no problem, you can always eat it,' said Lucy, sticking her tongue out and licking her top lip.

'I wouldn't if I were you,' said Izzie. 'Raw egg can give you that salmonella disease.'

'That's quite rare,' said TJ. 'And I think the egg has to be off.'

TJ's our resident medical adviser on account of the fact that both her parents are doctors and some of their medical knowledge rubs off on her.

Lucy quickly put her tongue back in her mouth. 'Yuck,' she said.

Izzie took her trainers off, put a towel in the bath, then got in and lay down with her feet resting up on the taps. 'Honestly, the things we girls have to do to look beautiful,' she said. 'I bet boys never do anything like this.'

'Don't you believe it,' said Lucy. 'Steve and Lal are always slapping moisturiser all over them. And they take an age in the bathroom getting ready. Boys can be just as vain as girls.'

'At least we don't have to shave,' said TJ.

'Well, not our faces,' I said. 'But we do our legs and under our arms. Waxing is better than shaving though, it lasts longer.'

'My gran does her chin,' TJ added, laughing. 'She said it's one of the awful things about getting old. Hair starts sprouting everywhere, from your ears, your nose, your chin.'

'Oo, sexy,' I said. I took a close look at my nostrils in the mirror. 'I hope that never happens to me.'

After we'd rinsed off our face masks, we resumed our discussion in Lucy's bedroom about the local boys. What Izzie had said about me judging by externals had irked me. I wasn't so superficial as to only go out with boys because of what they looked like or if they had money or something. My last long-term boyfriend had been very rich, but that wasn't the reason I went out with him. I liked him for who he was. That is until he dumped me because he was going to university in Scotland and wanted to be free to date any new girl that he fancied up there. Maybe the girls think I only dated him because he was loaded. I decided to find out what they really thought about me, but planned to ask them in a really subtle way.

'So Izzie, about what you said before. Were you saying that you think I'm shallow?' Oops, I thought. I knew before I'd finished the question that it hadn't come out the way I intended. Subtlety was never my best trait.

Izzie laughed. 'No Nesta, not shallow, but image is very important to you.'

'Like it isn't to you?' I asked. I looked at my three friends all busy painting each other's toenails. Lucy's petite and blonde, TJ and Iz are tall and dark and all three of them are gorgeous in their own ways, but they all work at it, forever trying new things and new looks in an attempt to improve on nature. I am *not* the only one. 'And Iz, you did a whole makeover on yourself just before term started in September.'

'I know. It's important to all of us,' she said as she began to paint TJ's toenails a purple shade called Vampire. 'All I was saying is that there is other stuff that's important as well. Like, what's inside a person.'

'I know that. TJ, Lucy, do you think I'm shallow?'

'I never said I thought you were shallow,' said Izzie. 'You did.'

'Yeah, but you think it,' I said, looking at TJ and Lucy.

Lucy looked uncomfortable. She hates confrontation, but I had to know what my friends really thought of me.

'I wouldn't use the word shallow,' she said after a few minutes, 'but I know a certain sense of style and looking good is important to you.'

'TJ?'

'Um. God. I don't know,' she said. 'You've obviously got a good brain or else you wouldn't do so well at school.'

'Yeah, but am I shallow?'

'Depends what you mean by shallow,' blustered TJ. 'I mean, I wouldn't say you're deep . . . but you're not shallow either.'

'Who wants to be deep,' I said lowering my voice. '*Bor*-ring.'

'I think Izzie's deep,' said Lucy, 'and she's far from boring. She's always thinking about things and asking questions about stuff like why we're here and what it's all about. You're not boring, Izzie.'

Oh, here we go. Now I've managed to insult one of my best friends. Me and my big mouth, I thought. I didn't mean to say that Izzie was boring. I'd better try and say something to make it clear what I really meant.

'Yeah and where does that get you, Izzie?' I asked. 'Who knows the answers to questions like that? You could drive yourself mad asking about life, the universe and everything. Perhaps that's why you are a bit mad. I reckon, we're here, you get on with it. End of story.'

Oops, I thought as Izzie's face fell. I don't think that helped. Maybe I should shut up for a while.

'That's it,' said TJ. 'Pragmatic. That's what you are, Nesta.'

Bugger, I thought. I don't know what pragmatic means. But no way am I going to let on or else they really will think that I'm shallow. Whatever it meant, I felt I was being got at. Huh.

'Right, pragmatic, I guess that's OK.'

'Yeah,' continued TJ, 'you just get on with life without questioning it too much. You like to have fun, do girlie things, enjoy life, you're not a complicated person and you're not that bothered about educating your mind or anything.'

'I am too. I read. I keep up with what's happening.'

TJ and Izzie burst out laughing. 'OK, what have you read lately?' asked TJ.

'*CosmoGIRL! Bliss. OK!* magazine.'

TJ and Izzie exchanged glances.

'What's wrong with that?' I asked.

'Nothing,' said Izzie. 'We all read the mags and they're great. But when did you last read a book?'

'All the time. We read books every day at school. There's a time and a place for everything. And school is the place for books. Out of school is the place for fun.'

'But some books *are* fun,' said TJ. 'They can take you to different places, let you in to different people's experiences, how others think. Don't close your mind to them just because they're not all glossy with photos of celebrities in them.'

I was definitely being got at. TJ is a regular bookworm. She reads everything and anything and Izzie's dad lectures in English at some university in town and is always giving her heavy-looking books to read. Not my cup of tea at all, I'd rather watch a good soap on telly, but she dutifully reads everything her dad gives her.

'OK,' I said, 'so I'm not a bookworm. That doesn't make me shallow. Lucy doesn't read a lot, do you Luce?'

Lucy looked more uncomfortable than ever now. 'Actually, Steve passes on some of his books to me and I quite often read late at night.'

'Hah! Closet reader,' I said. 'I never knew that.'

'You never asked,' said Lucy blushing furiously. 'And I didn't think you'd be interested.'

'Hhmmm. So you think I'm too shallow to have a discussion about books.'

'No,' TJ and Lucy chorused.

'Well, I didn't know I had such nerdy brainbox friends,' I said.

'See, that's just it,' said Izzie. 'You think that because someone reads that they're a nerd. You couldn't be more wrong.'

'Huh,' I said.

'I think,' said TJ, 'you have different people for different parts of yourself. Like I can talk to Izzie about books, astrology and stuff like what life is all about, I can talk to Lucy about fashion and design and I can talk to you about . . . er, make-up and . . . or . . . I know, advice about boys. Nobody knows more about boys than you, Nesta.'

Well that's true, I thought. I suppose it helps having an older brother. Boys have never phased me. I sussed out pretty early that all of them, no matter what age or how cool they act, are little boys underneath. They are as nervous and unsure about girls as girls are about them.

'So,' I said. 'We have here, Izzie the seeker, TJ the thinker, Lucy the designer *extraordinaire* and me, the what? The airhead?'

'Course not,' said Lucy. 'No one said that. What's got into you today? You always come in the top ten in exams at school, so how can you think that you're an airhead? You're the one putting yourself down.'

'And you are the boy expert,' said TJ.

'OK then,' I said, 'when it comes to boys. Fact. The cute ones often don't read because they have got a life. Fact. The nerdy ones bury their heads in books because they haven't got a life.'

'*Noooo*,' said Izzie. 'No way. You couldn't be more wrong. I mean, take Ben. He's cute and reads loads.'

Hmm, I thought. Ben is Izzie's ex and although really nice, not someone I'd call a babe magnet. Definitely not my type.

'Well, I think there are two types of boys,' I said. 'The hot babe magnets who, OK, might be trouble and break your heart, but are fun and great to be seen out with. And there's the other type, not quite as attractive, but cosy and good company and you know where you are with them, because they don't mess you around, basically because they know that if they did, they might not get off with anyone else.'

Izzie laughed. 'You always see things in black or white. Nothing in between.'

'So?'

'You can't always generalise, especially about people,' said TJ. 'I don't think everything is black or white. I think there are shades of grey as well. Like take Steve, he's really clever and also attractive.'

I kept my mouth shut. Steve is one of Lucy's brothers and he's been dating TJ for ages now. But once again, like Ben, yes, nice, a laugh, but babe magnet – no way. I didn't want to insult TJ by saying that her boyfriend wasn't a babe, nor Lucy by saying that I didn't think her brother was attractive. People can be very defensive about their family. It's like they can say the worst possible things themselves about brothers and sisters, but God help anyone else who says anything bad. I guess I'm the same about my brother, Tony. I slag him off something rotten sometimes, but I won't hear a word against him from anyone else. I dutifully kept my mouth zipped about Steve, but sometimes it's difficult holding in what I really think. Sometimes I worry that I might be getting that disease, Tourette's syndrome or something. I read about it in a magazine. Instead of blood leaking out or people being sick, people puke out their thoughts instead and they shout awful things in public or on the tube or somewhere. They can't help it apparently, like the 'What not to say and when not to say it' filter is missing from their brain. I'd be forever in trouble if my thoughts leaked out. I wonder if it's possible to have inner Tourette's syndrome. Sometimes I think awful things about people before I can stop myself. Mad things just pop into my head. Sometimes my thoughts shock even me. In school sometimes, I want to shout 'knickers' at inappropriate moments like school assembly when our headmistress is droning on. Or if I see someone really unattractive in the street, I think, 'Woah, there goes a fat ugly one,' then I feel awful because some people can't help the way they look. Or when Dad is giving me a hard time about something, I think, 'Hhmm. Take your advice, Pater, and stick it up your bum.' Luckily, most of the time my brain filter works and I manage to keep my thoughts to myself. Maybe I'm secretly insane? It is a worry.

'So you reckon the choices are gorgeous and dangerous versus safe and secure, but not so gorgeous?' asked Lucy.

'Yeah,' I said. 'That's your choice. One or the other.'

'I reckon you can get boys who are both,' said Izzie. 'Gorgeous and safe and secure. Not all gorgeous boys mess you around.'

'They might not at first,' I said, thinking about Simon dumping me, 'but they do in the end, basically because they know they can.'

TJ shook her head. 'I agree with Izzie,' she said.

'Lucy?' I asked.

She's had this on/off thing with my brother Tony for over a year. Even though he's my brother, I can see that he's the first type, ie: is v.v. attractive even though a little arrogant with it. There's always a queue of girls after him and he never gets serious about any of them. Except Lucy that is. He really likes her, but half the reason that he stays interested is because she doesn't fall over herself wanting to be with him. She keeps him on his toes. I know for a fact that if she wasn't messing him around, he'd be messing her around. It's like they're doing a dance, he steps forward, she steps back. She steps forward, he steps back. Right now, in the dance, Lucy is stepping back and Tony is stepping forward.

'Um, I also agree with Izzie,' said Lucy. 'Oh, I know Tony's not exactly Mr Commitment, but at least he's honest about who he is.'

'Yeah, course,' said Izzie. 'There are all sorts of types. There are boys who are deep *and* gorgeous. Cute boys who think about things. Cute boys who will commit and not mess you around. People are different depending on who they're with, so maybe you just haven't brought out the deeper side of the boys you've been with.'

'What do you mean?' I asked.

'Well, like we're different with different people,' said Izzie. 'You're one way with your parents, another way with teachers, another way with your friends, another way with boys.'

'Yeah. So?'

'Well, like TJ was saying, she talks to Iz about some things, Lucy about others and you about others.'

'Yeah,' said TJ. 'Like I go to Iz for advice and I come to you for a laugh.'

I had to think about that. Was that a compliment or an insult?

'Are you saying you don't think I can give advice?'

'No . . . yes,' said TJ looking flustered. 'I was trying to say something nice about you. Not many people are as much fun as you. Oh, I don't know. I think you're being over sensitive today, Nesta.'

'Yes, don't be a drama queen,' said Izzie.

I'm not even going to reply to that, I thought. Drama queen! *Moi?* As *if*.

'All I was saying,' continued Izzie, 'was that we're probably totally different with different boys too. With some, you don't feel yourself at all and have nothing to say, with others, you can't stop talking. People bring out different sides of you. Maybe you've never brought out what you call the nerdy side of a boy, because you've never talked about anything to bring it out.'

'So you *are* saying I'm shallow and I bring out the shallow part of people, boys included. *And* I can't give advice. *And* I'm a drama queen.'

'*No*,' said Izzie. 'Oh, I don't know. Just maybe, next time you like a boy, try talking about a book you've read or ask him what he feels about the purpose of life or something.'

Huh, I thought, not exactly a fun chat-up line in my estimation. I was feeling peeved by what the girls had said. I don't want to be thought of as an airhead-type drama queen bimbo. I'm not. I do well at school. I *do* think about things. Like, what to wear, how to do my hair, which is my favourite boy band and so on. But maybe I should talk about 'deep' stuff. Books. Um. Maybe I'd better read one – a grown-up one, that is. I used to read a lot when I was younger, but I went off it. I don't know why. I'll start again when I get home, I decided. I'll pick a really intellectual, impressive-type book and that will show them, when I start quoting bits off by heart. Then I'll find a boy and knock his socks off with my brainy brain-type brain as well as my looks. I shall show them all that airhead, I am not.

Lucy's DIY Face-masks

Egg and Yeast Mask

1 egg yolk

1 tablespoon of brewer's yeast

1 teaspoon of sunflower oil

Mix into a smooth paste. Apply to face and neck and leave for fifteen minutes then rinse off.

NB: *The yeast can stimulate the skin and draw out impurities, so not the best one to use before a big party in case it brings out any lurking spots.*

Nourishing Mask

1 whole egg

1 teaspoon honey

1 teaspoon almond oil

Mix together then apply. Leave on for fifteen minutes then rinse off.

Rejuvenating Mask

2 tablespoons of ripe avocado

1 teaspoon honey

3 drops of lemon juice

Mash the avocado, add the lemon juice, add the honey and mix into a paste. Apply and leave on for at least twenty minutes. You may have to lie on the floor with a towel behind your head and neck for this one as it can be a bit runny.

Banana Mask *(especially good for dry skin)*

Half a ripe banana

1 tablespoon of honey

1 tablespoon of double cream

Mash the banana. Mix with the honey and cream and apply.

(This one's OK to eat as well!)

Chapter 2

War Zone

When I got home later that afternoon, I intended to go straight to the dictionary and look up pragmatic then go and find myself a 'deep' book from the shelves in our sitting room. However, as soon as I'd stepped into the hall of our flat, I heard raised voices coming from the kitchen. Oops, war zone, I thought as I went in to see what it was all about.

'But Dad,' Tony was saying, 'everyone in our year is taking their test and Mark Janson has even got his own car.'

Dad looked tight-lipped. 'I said no, and that's final. We'll talk about it again when you're nineteen.'

Ah, I thought, I know what this is about. It's Tony's birthday tomorrow. September 22nd. He'll be eighteen and he wants to do a course of driving lessons in the hope of getting a car when he passes his A-levels. He did ask if he could learn to drive last year when he was seventeen and I remember that there were fireworks then. It's weird because Dad is usually pretty cool about most things, but when it comes to talking about driving, he clamps up and becomes totally unapproachable. Poor Tony, he really thought Dad would give in this year and had even saved all his cash Christmas presents to go towards lessons.

I decided to step in and help.

'Don't be a meanie, Dad. It *is* his eighteenth birthday, that's a really special one.' Well that clearly didn't help, I thought as Dad's expression turned from frosty to ice. However, I don't believe in giving up easily. 'Loads of people Tony's age drive, Dad. And Tony would be very careful, wouldn't you?'

'Yeah, course.'

'He may be careful, but there are some maniacs out on the road,' said Dad.

'But . . .' Tony began.

'I *said* end of story,' said Dad, then he got up and left the room.

'Sorry,' I said as Tony sat at the counter and put his head in his hands.

'It's not fair,' he groaned.

'You sound like Kevin,' I said laughing and went into my impersonation of the teenage character that Harry Enfield plays in the film *Kevin and Perry Go Large*. He's a really obnoxious fifteen-year-old who is always telling his parents, 'It's not fair,' and 'I hate you.' It usually makes Tony laugh when I do it, but this time he wasn't going for it.

'It makes me look like a right dork,' he said. 'Three of my mates have been driving for six months already. I hate being the one who has to act like a kid – oh my dad won't let me. It sounds so pathetic.'

'So what *do* you want to do on your birthday?' When someone is feeling low, my philosophy is to change the subject to something cheerful.

'Not much I can do, is there? On a Monday? Mum says we can do something special at a later date, maybe a weekend when everyone's a bit more chilled.'

'But you have to do something on the day and although, yeah, you have to go to school, there's always the evening. You could do something nice if Mum hasn't already got something planned.'

'Actually she did say we could go out for dinner tomorrow, but who wants to go out with old misery Dad? Not exactly exciting. I'll probably meet up with some mates after school. You can come if you promise not to drool on any of them.'

'As if. Anyway I've got a dentist's appointment after school tomorrow,' I said. 'I might not be up to eating out if I have to have a filling or something. Why don't you have a party later? It is your eighteenth after all.'

Tony shook his head. 'That's what Mum said. I'll think

about it, but if Mum and Dad want to supervise, I'd rather not.'

'So what would you really like to do?'

Tony was quiet while he thought. 'I know what I'd like to do,' he said finally. 'I'd like to go out with Lucy. Just the two of us. Not actually on my birthday necessarily, but some time soon after. But I don't suppose she'll be up for a date either, you know what she's like, always blowing hot and cold.'

'Ahh,' I said, putting on my moany groany voice. 'Poor Tony. Itthh noooot faaiiirrr.'

At least this time he laughed. Or grimaced, sometimes it's hard to tell with Tone.

A few minutes later Mum came through. 'Ah good. I'm glad to get you both together as I wanted to have a bit of a chat.'

Tony and I looked at each other and tried not to laugh. Quite a few of our mates' parents have been doing this lately, so we knew what to expect by 'a bit of a chat'. It was a talk about sex, drugs or drink and how we mustn't do any of them.

'So,' she began, 'just to let you know how things are at the moment.'

Ah. Maybe I was wrong, I thought. Maybe it's not the 'It only takes one time and, before you know it, you're pregnant' sex lecture. Maybe it's the 'We have to tighten our belts' lecture.

'As you know,' Mum continued, 'my contract at the station was renewed last year . . .'

'Oh, they're not talking about letting you go again are they?' asked Tony.

Earlier this year, Mum thought she was going to be out of a job. She works as a news presenter on Cable and her position, as with all the presenters, is precarious as the producers like to try out new faces or, as Mum says, younger faces.

'No, they aren't talking of getting rid of me, no, just cutting down my hours. The producers are doing it to all us diehards and, to give them their due, they do have to keep trying out new people. So. This is the situation. Dad's got a new film to direct and that's going well, but there's not an enormous budget on this one and he's doing it mainly because of the prestige, not the money. It will look good on his CV and hopefully lead to other things. So money's going to be a bit tight, plus we'll have a big tax bill coming in January. So. What does this mean for all of us? Bit of budgeting. Pulling our belts in a little and no money for extras I'm afraid. I know there was a skiing trip you fancied going on with the school, Tony, but that's out for the time being. But we can live, that's the main thing.'

'That's cool,' said Tony. 'I wasn't that bothered about skiing to be honest. Not since Mark Crawley broke both his arm and leg on the last trip. Seeing him lumber about in a plaster cast put me off a bit.'

'And I'm sorry, Tony,' said Mum. 'About the party for your eighteenth. Do you mind waiting a while? Until things have improved a bit?'

'No problem,' said Tony. 'I wasn't sure I wanted one anyway.'

He's great with Mum. They have a really good relationship, much better than he has with Dad, which is interesting seeing as Dad is his real dad, but Mum is his stepmum. His real mum died when he was tiny, then later Dad married my mum. She's always been there as long as he can remember. Our family confuses a lot of people, because Dad is Italian – dark-haired, dark-eyed, olive-skinned. (Actually he's three-quarters Italian and a quarter Spanish to be precise as Granddad is half Italian, half Spanish and Grandma is Italian.) Tony's inherited his European good looks, complete with Dad's movie star type dimple on his chin. Mum's Jamaican, dark skin, dark hair, green eyes and, although I take after her, I'm not as dark, more kind of coffee coloured. When new people meet Tony and me, then find out that we're brother and sister, you can see their minds working overtime trying to work out why we look so different.

'OK, Nesta?' asked Mum.

'Yeah. You know me,' I said. 'I don't care in the least about material things.' Mum did a double-take and Tony burst out laughing. What a cheek. I am clearly one of the most misunderstood people in the history of time. Still, at least what Mum had said explained why Dad was being funny about Tony having driving lessons. Clearly he couldn't afford them, but didn't want to admit it. Men or boys, the whole male species are weird about some things and can't just come out and say stuff like they're lost or broke or something. As if to admit you're hard up means you've failed in some way. Huh, I thought, I have no problem admitting when I have no money.

'So we're poor again, are we?' I asked.

'Not poor, Nesta,' said Mum. 'Just not rich at the moment.'

We're always going through these phases – spare money, no spare money. Dad says working in the media is often feast or famine. When I'm an actress, I'm going to make sure I'm mega rich all the time by getting into every play and film going, as I don't reckon it's much fun having no dosh. I can see what a strain the ups and downs of finances put on Mum and Dad.

'Anything you want to ask?' asked Mum.

Tony shook his head.

'Nah,' I said. I planned to go upstairs and learn my audition part for the end of term play at school. We're doing *West Side Story* this year and I want to go for the part of Maria.

'Good,' said Mum. 'So you both understand? No extras for a while?'

I nodded. It's funny, I quite like the fact that Mum

treats Tony and me like adults and keeps us informed as to what's going on, as I know some people's parents don't. It makes me feel accepted as a grown-up. On the other hand, I don't want to know, because I reckon all that stuff is their job, being parents, paying the bills and all that and I want to just be a teenager and not think about any of it. Mum says she tells us about the finances so that we don't think that 'Money grows on trees'. As if.

'Er, Matt, wasn't there something you wanted to say?' Mum called into the hall, then turned back to us. 'And your dad had something he wanted to say as well.'

Ah. Now the sex talk, I thought, sneaking a glance at Tony. He raised an eyebrow as if to say, this should be interesting.

There was a cough from somewhere in the vicinity of the sitting room, then we heard Dad's footsteps approaching.

He shuffled about on his feet for a few moments. 'Right,' he said. 'Ahem. Yes. Er . . . I . . . I wanted to talk to you about contraception.'

'What! *Again?*' Tony groaned.

I rolled my eyes. 'Mum, Dad. We do all this stuff at school.'

'Yeah,' said Tony as he leaned back on his stool and put his hands behind his head in that arrogant 'You can't teach me anything' way of his. 'But it's cool, if you want to talk about it. So . . . Dad. Contraception? What would you like to know?'

I creased up laughing. So did Mum and Dad. Phew. War zone safe for a few more days.

Pragmatic: dealing with matters according to their practical significance or immediate importance.

Chapter 3

Count-down to Clamming up

Fifty-eight, fifty-nine, sixty. Four minutes left. One, two, three . . . I counted as I lay on the couch at the dentist's the next day after school. About four more minutes and I should be out of here, I thought, then it's all over for another six months. Dental surgeries are *not* my favourite places: the persistent buzz of drilling behind closed doors, the smell of polished wood mixed with antiseptic mouthwash, the anguished screams of despair as patients beg for mercy . . . OK, maybe the screams are in my head, but it doesn't help that my dentist, Mr Saltman, has a poster of Steve Martin in the film, *Little Shop of Horrors*, on his ceiling. Everyone that lies back on the chair has no choice but to see the poster as Mr Saltman works on their teeth. In the film, Steve Martin plays Orin Scrivello, the demented and sadistic dentist. Hhmm? What is Mr Saltman trying to say to his patients, I wondered.

'Scange choich of poh – er,' I mumbled as I pointed up at the ceiling. I was trying to say, strange choice of poster, but it was somewhat difficult with Mr Saltman's thumb and index finger in my cheek and my top lip stretched almost up to my ear (not my most alluring look). As he tapped my teeth with some cold metal implement, I closed my eyes and tried to think of nice relaxing things. Izzie had briefed me as we were leaving school. 'Think soothing thoughts,' she'd said, 'positive visualisations to distract you from the pain.' She'd suggested waterfalls, flowers, dolphins. Sadly dolphins don't do it for me, nor waterfalls, *bor*-ring. I decided to try and think up some soothing visualisations of my own. Things that made me happy to think about. The perfume counters in Selfridges. Rails of fab clothes in Morgan. The lingerie department in Fenwicks. Snogging Brad Pitt. Oh, I'm being shallow, I suddenly thought. Clothes, underwear, snogging. No, I can do better than that. I can do deep visualisations or else the girls would have been right yesterday, all I think about is my appearance, boys and clothes. No, I'll try again. I *will* think deep meaningful things. I imagined myself going on a protest march to save the environment. Hhmm, I wondered, what does one wear for a demonstration? Green or brown? Something that looks like you're serious about the cause, but casually alluring as well in case there's a hot eco-warrior boy there. Oh *no*. I was back to clothes and boys. I tried again. Think uplifting thoughts, uplifting, *deep* thoughts, I told myself. Something to distract from the fact that my jaw has locked and my neck muscles have gone into spasm. No. The visualisation stuff wasn't working. All I could see now was Steve Martin with his drill in his hand, an evil look in his eye and he was coming closer. I was never very good at getting the right visualisation for the right moment, I'm not like Izzie, she's so into all that New Age hocus pocus and it seems to work for her.

I opened my eyes to see if Mr Saltman had finished. No. He was still nose to nose with me, only with a mask over his nose and mouth. And glasses over his eyes. He looked like a giant insect hovering in my face and suddenly I had the urge to laugh as the words to Steve Martin's song from the film rang through my brain, 'to beee a dena-tist . . .' Gulp. Arghh, I thought as I struggled to swallow.

'Ow,' I cried as Mr Saltman pulled my mouth to the left. Real person down here, I thought, skin may be elastic, but it's not *that* stretchy. Sadly he didn't seem to be picking up on my thoughts and continued to yank my bottom lip as though it was made out of plasticine.

'So Nesta, have you been flossing regularly?' he asked.

'Urg, argle oof,' I attempted to say. I mean how ridiculous? Asking people questions when they're lying on their backs with their mouths full of fingers, metal things and cotton wool. I think it may be one way that dentists make their jobs enjoyable. When they get bored or something, they wait until someone is in their chair with their mouth full of dentisty type stuff, then they ask them questions and secretly laugh as they watch their patients struggling to answer.

I nodded, then tried to swallow again. Not long to go now, surely? Two more minutes. One, two, three, four . . .

Finally Mr Saltman stood back. 'OK, you can rinse now,' he said as he pressed a button on the side of the chair causing it to suddenly jerk up from horizontal to vertical and so throwing me forward. That's the other way that dentists get their laughs, I decided. Playing around with their chairs. Most of them have some way of lowering you down or pushing you back up. I wonder if they have ejector buttons for really difficult patients or nasty kids who bite them. They can just press a secret button and the patient flies out of the chair and back into reception. I know I'd have one fitted if I were a dentist. But then, I'm not going to be a dentist. I'm going to be an actress, which is one of the reasons I do actually turn up regularly for this torture. It's v. important to have good teeth. Which reminds me, I ought to be going over my audition piece for *West Side Story*. I'd decided to do Maria's song, 'There's a Place For Us'. Pah, I thought, I could have been doing that as a distraction. It would have been a great visualisation, imagining that I'd got the lead part and I was there, on stage, singing my heart out as everyone looked on in admiration.

As I rinsed with the disgusting bright pink liquid in the plastic cup on the stand next to the chair, Mr Saltman went to look at the X-rays of my teeth that he'd taken earlier. He started whispering to his assistant, a girl who looked younger than I do. No way she's coming anywhere near my mouth, I thought, she's clearly only just got her second teeth herself.

'So do they all have to come out?' I asked. I thought I was being very funny, but Mr Saltman wasn't laughing.

'No, none will have to come out, I don't think,' he said. 'But I *am* concerned about the slight overcrowding in your mouth. It might cause a crossover on the top two teeth as you get older and possibly on the bottom ones too. It won't be evident for a while but will happen . . .'

What is he talking about, I wondered? Crossovers. Overcrowding. 'Uh?' I asked.

'We'll need to get an impression of your teeth,' he said.

'There you go.' I beamed, giving him my widest smile.

Mr Saltman laughed. 'No, not that kind of impression. I need a moulding to send to Mr Schneider, the orthodontist.'

'For what?'

'You need to have a brace fitted, Nesta.'

'A whadttttt!!?'

'Brace,' said Mr Saltman. 'There's a chance if we leave them that some of the front teeth will grow crooked. A brace will soon correct that, then you'll have picture perfect peggies for when you're older.'

'But I'm fifteen, Mr Saltman.'

'I know,' he smiled. 'Perfect time for the corrections.'

Perfect time to ruin my life, I thought. Perfect time to ruin my appearance. My pulling power. My social life. My snogging skills. My . . . ohmigod, my *part* in *West Side Story*. No way can I go for the part of Maria. I'd be the laughing stock as soon as I opened my mouth to sing. In fact, instead of singing, 'There's a Place For Us', I'd have to sing, 'There's a Brace For Us'.

'No. I can't have a brace,' I said firmly. 'No, take all my teeth out and give me false ones. At least that way, I can still smile.'

Mr Saltman laughed again. 'It will only be for a year, Nesta. And so many people your age have them these days.'

Yes, but I'm not so many people, I thought.

'It won't be so bad,' continued Mr Saltman, 'and Mr Schneider will keep a close eye on you. You'll need to go for regular check-ups every few weeks.'

Nooooooooooooooooooooooooooooo, I moaned inwardly. I thought I was through with dentists until the next check-up in six months. As I lay on the chair inwardly going through how my life was going to change, Mr Saltman's assistant had been out, then come back with what looked like a piece of plasticine on a tray. She put it in front of me.

'Oh dinner? No thanks,' I said holding my hand up. 'I'll pass.'

Mr Saltman held the gloop close to my mouth.

'Now bite in,' he said, 'and we'll get a nice imprint of your teeth.'

Dutifully I bit into the minty flavoured putty.

'Good girl,' said Mr Saltman. 'Now hold still until I say.'

That's it, I thought. My life is over. I shall never go out again. I shall do a Harry Potter and I don't mean go to Hogwart's and become a wizard. No, I shall voluntarily move into a cupboard under the stairs and not speak to anyone. Never show my face. Not for a year. Not until I can smile again. So the girls were right, I thought. I am shallow. I *do* care a lot about my appearance. I can't help it. I like boys noticing me. I like looking good. And now what? Who's going to give me a second look except to say, oh how awful. Have you SEEN that girl's metal teeth? And as for my stage career, this has put an end to all that for a while. No way I'm putting myself in the spotlight now. Huh. Life stinks.

As I waited for the impression to take, I glanced up at the poster of Steve Martin. I could swear he gave me a satisfied smile.

Izzie's Visualisation To Take Your Mind Off Bad Times

1) Lie back, close your eyes, uncross your legs and arms. Take three deep breaths right into your abdomen.
2) Think of a time when you were totally relaxed, confident and happy, perhaps by a beach or a river or in the garden in summer.
3) Visualise the colours in your scene, now turn them up, make them brighter in your mind.
4) Imagine the sounds: birds singing, leaves rustling or waves breaking on the shore. Turn the sounds up in your mind.
5) Imagine the smells: fresh cut grass, the scent of roses or the salty air at the sea. Turn the scents up in your mind.
6) Bring all the sounds, scents and sights together into a whole picture in your mind.
7) Fix this picture with a physical sign, ie: when you have the picture clear in your mind, make a gesture with your hands, either touch the thumb and index finger together or clench your fist. Every time you do this gesture in future, it will remind you of your positive feel-good visualisation and take you to a cool state of mind quickly.

Nesta's Visualisation For Relaxation

Forget Izzie's version. *Way* too complicated.

1) Lie back, close eyes. Imagine snogging your fave boy band pin-up and he's the best kisser you've ever come across in your whole life. May also help to imagine that you look your tip-top best at the time.

Chapter 4

Tragic Heroine

Waiting for the date for the brace to be put in was like waiting for exam results and three very looooong weeks later, the dreaded deed was done. On Monday afternoon I went, like a man doomed to the guillotine, resigned to my terrible fate and, though I tried to be brave, even my snogging fantasy didn't help. I emerged from the orthodontist's looking to the world a normal teenager, but inside I was a wounded soul, cut down in the prime of my life. I returned home to take refuge in the only place where I would find solace for the next year. Under my duvet.

As soon as school was out, the crowds had gathered to mock.

'Come on, let us in,' called Izzie through my bedroom door.

'Yeah, you can't look that bad,' said Lucy.

'Yeah, come on Nesta,' said TJ. 'It's no big deal, honestly. Loads of people in school have them nowadays.'

'Yeah and loads of people have spots,' I called back. 'Doesn't mean I have to join them.'

Suddenly I heard a scuffle in the corridor outside my room, then Tony's voice, some stifled giggles, then footsteps retreating. Well, it didn't take them long to give up, I thought as I lay back on my bed in my best tragic heroine pose. When things are bad in my life, I sometimes try and pretend that I'm a character in a film and act through the feelings I'm experiencing. I racked my brains for an appropriate role. Heroine with a brace? Julia Roberts? Sandra Bullock? J-Lo? Hhmm? Parts with braces? Parts with braces? No, the only role that kept coming back was Anthony Hopkins as Hannibal Lecter in *Silence of the Lambs*, when he's in prison and has to wear a metal contraption over his jaw to stop him eating people.

I got up and went to the door to listen for clues as to what my mates were up to. Silence. Huh, I thought. Abandoned in my hour of need. I know I wouldn't let them in my room, but they should know well enough by now that I would have done in a few minutes. I just wanted them to appreciate how upsetting this all was. I'd been putting on a very brave face for the last few weeks since I heard I had to have a brace. Laughing it off, saying it was no big deal, I didn't care, etc. All lies, so that they wouldn't think that I was vain or shallow. But now it was in, on, or whatever, I couldn't keep up the act. I needed my mates to commiserate with and tell me that it was all going to be all right. I did care. It *did* hurt. Not so much when it was fitted, but afterwards. Strange and sharp in my mouth. Uncomfortable for a few days is what Mr Schneider had told me it would feel like. *Uncomfortable!* I think he needs to check his dictionary definitions. This isn't uncomfortable, it's agony, my gums ache like anything. And it didn't help that the first person I bumped into when I came out of Mr Scheider's surgery was Michael Brenman from Year Twelve. We had a very brief thing once (a snog) and he gave me a big flirty smile when he saw me. Course, all I saw were his perfect, white, straight teeth. I clamped my lips together and ran. Oh misery, I thought, is this what it's going to be like for the next year? Year. *Year?* That's three hundred and sixty-five days. Twelve months, fifty-two weeks of not being able to open my mouth when a cute boy is around. If ever there was a hell on earth, *this* is it.

I could hear footsteps returning, so I unlocked my door then leaped back on to the bed. Someone tried the handle, then on seeing that the door wasn't locked any more, Izzie stuck her head round. When she saw me lying there, she opened the door wide. Lucy, Izzie, TJ and Tony all stood in the frame of the doorway giggling like five-year-olds. Then they smiled. They all looked like they had no teeth.

I cracked up. Even though I'd been determined to keep up my tragic heroine act a little longer, I had to laugh (though I made sure I put my hand over my mouth as I did).

'All for one and one for all,' a toothless Lucy said with a grin.

'How did you do that?' I asked from behind my hand.

'Drinking chocolate,' said Tony. 'You put some in your mouth then sort of mush it up a bit, then put it on your teeth with your tongue.'

'Just to show that you're not alone,' said TJ.

'Hey, come on,' I said. 'I still have my teeth! It's only a brace.'

Izzie rubbed her tongue along her front teeth, turning them back to white. 'Exactly,' she said, then came over to sit next to me on the bed. 'So come on, give us a look.'

The others crowded round and stared at me, like they were waiting for a circus freak to begin his act. I shook my head.

'You're going to have to open your mouth sometime,' said Lucy. 'Come on, put your hand down.'

I shook my head again. 'It's horrible.'

'OK, then we'll all have to start talking like you, with

our hands over our mouths,' said Lucy. 'We'll start a new craze.'

They all started messing about, talking with their hands over their mouths. Maybe it's not so bad, I thought as I watched them all having a laugh. Maybe I can risk it.

'OK, I'll give you a quick look,' I said. I moved my hand away from my face, then attempted a smile.

Mistake. Not even Izzie was fast enough to cover her shocked reaction. '*Woah*,' she said.

'Wow,' said Lucy coming closer and staring at my teeth. 'Did it hurt a *lot*?'

'More now than when he put it on. It's kind of sore,' I said as I put my hand back over my mouth. 'My whole mouth aches. Does it look like . . . totally awful?'

By now Izzie had recovered. 'No, not *totally* awful. Just a shock at first as we're not used to it. But it's OK. And it's not the end of the world . . . You still look fabulous . . .'

'As long as I keep my mouth shut?'

Izzie nodded, then burst out laughing. 'Sorry, sorry,' she blustered, 'just people are always telling you to keep your mouth shut and now you're going to. Sorry. I wouldn't laugh if you were really hurt or something . . .'

I gave her arm a light slap. 'It's OK. I guess I wouldn't want you lying to me. I know it looks weird. They're called railway tracks because that's what they look like. I could have got coloured ones if I'd wanted, but I didn't want to draw more attention to them than necessary.'

'I don't know,' said TJ, 'Mary O'Connor has got pink and purple ones, I think they look really cool.'

'There's a brace for us,' sang Lucy to the tune of 'There's a Place For Us' from *West Side Story*. 'Somewhere . . . a brace for us.' They'd all thought it was really funny when I'd told them of my version of the song and hadn't stopped singing it since, whenever they saw me, in fact.

'A brace is a brace is a brace, whatever colour it is,' I said.

'Not necessarily,' said Tony. 'Henry, a guy at our school, has a Tom Cruise.'

'Which is?' I asked.

'An invisible brace, transparent. Apparently Tom Cruise had one but they cost a fortune. Henry's parents are loaded though.'

'It will be all right,' said Lucy. 'You'll get used to it soon. It's like when you have a bad haircut, you feel you can never go out again but you do.'

'That's because your hair grows again,' I said.

'No,' Lucy insisted. 'It's because you get used to it.'

'Yeah,' said Izzie, 'and you have so much else going for you, great legs, great body, great hair. No one will ever even notice your teeth.'

Their words of support weren't helping. 'No boy will ever fancy me again,' I said with a groan. 'I will have to live the life of a nun for a year like Julie Andrews in *The Sound of Music*.'

Lucy picked up a towel from the chest of drawers and

put it over her head. 'Cliiiimb eveeeery mountaaaain, follow eeeevery streeeeam . . .' she warbled in a soprano voice.

'We thought you might want to go to Hampstead. Cruise the shops,' said TJ. 'Cheer you up a bit.'

'Can't,' I said, lying back on the bed. 'My former life is over.'

'Nah,' said Lucy. 'Something will happen. As Mum always says, life never closes a door without opening a window.'

I shook my head. 'Yeah, right. And there's light at the end of the tunnel.'

'That's the attitude,' said Izzie.

'Yeah. The light at the end of the tunnel is an oncoming train.'

Izzie laughed at our old joke. 'Oh, it will be all right,' she said.

'No it won't. From now on, I'm going to be a recluse.'

'OK,' said Izzie, lying next to me. 'We'll be recluses with you.'

Tony went to make hot chocolate for all of us (part of his trying-to-impress-Lucy act), then we lay around listening to sad songs about loneliness and generally feeling dejected. Even though I was really the only one who had anything to feel tragic about, it was nice that they tried to share it with me. Tony brought in an opera CD, which he said was about a real tragic heroine (as if I wasn't) singing about despair. However, by this time, I was beginning to get bored with moping about, and listening to the opera singer screeching away was the last straw.

'What I don't understand about opera,' I said, 'is why, just when the heroine discovers that she's about to die of some terrible lung disease, she sings her head off for another hour. Get on, die and put us all out of our misery, I say.'

'I'll second that,' said Lucy.

'So does this mean that you've had enough of being a recluse then?' asked TJ.

'Dunno, maybe,' I said. 'Yeah. Brace or no brace, this being tragic lark's a bit boring.'

'So what shall we do then?' asked Lucy.

'Movie,' said Izzie.

'Movie,' chorused TJ and Lucy.

Half an hour later, we were coming out of the local library with the DVD, *Godfather II*. TJ loves this film. She's seen it five times already, mainly because she's in love with Robert de Niro. Hmm. Each to their own, I thought, he's not my fave fantasy babe, *way* too old! Next stop was the pizza shop. This is more like it, I thought, as we made our way through the entrance hall of the library, you've got to still have fun, no matter what life throws at you.

Izzie stopped to look at the notices on the board. They advertise all sorts of the stuff that she's into. T'ai chi, crystal healing, astrology, massage.

'Hey, check this out,' she said as she scanned the board. 'It might be just the thing for you, Nesta.'

I went over to join her and read the notice.

> ***Acting for All.*** *Wednesday nights, 7–8.30. A fun and relaxed class given by a professional actor. Improvisation, drama games, vocal technique and script work. Everyone welcome from beginners to working actors wanting to refresh their skills. £5 per session.*

'Five quid,' said Izzie. 'That's cheap.'

'A lot of the council-run courses are,' said Lucy. 'My mum said they try to make them accessible for everyone.'

'Yeah,' I said, 'sounds good. And it would be good use of my brace time. I mean, no way I can perform in publico like in *West Side Story*, but to do a class away from school where I don't know anyone, that would be cool.'

'I still think that you should go for the part in *West Side Story*,' said Izzie.

'And I think you should stand on your head and wave your knickers in the air,' I replied, 'but neither of us are going to do it, are we?'

Izzie went to do a handstand right there, up against the wall in the library, but I pulled her back. 'No, no, I didn't mean it. But no way am I going for the part. I told you. I don't want anyone looking at me, but . . .' I glanced back at the noticeboard, 'this course looks interesting.'

'Yeah,' said TJ, 'but the people that do these courses are usually middle-aged and decrepit . . .'

'Exactly,' I said. 'No chance of humiliating myself in front of any cute boys of our age then. No, I think it will be brilliant. Just the thing. Excellento.'

Izzie laughed. 'You know what I love about you?'

'What?'

'The way you can go from total misery to total elation, all in the space of a day.'

'All in the space of five minutes sometimes.' I smiled back at her from behind my hand. I was feeling a million times better than earlier this afternoon. 'My mum says that when life throws you a lemon, you have to make lemonade. My brace is the lemon, doing this course would be making lemonade, if you know what I mean. It would be a way of using my time constructively. Only one thing would make it better . . .'

'What?' asked Lucy.

'If one of you guys would do the course as well.'

'Not me,' said TJ. 'I have to work on the school magazine Wednesday nights.'

'And I said I'd help Dad restock the shop on Wednesday nights this term,' said Lucy. Her dad runs the local health food shop and putting in some hours there is one way Lucy can pick up some spare cash. 'Sorry, Nesta.'

'No prob.' I turned to Izzie.

'But I don't want to be an actress,' she said heading for the door. 'I want to be a singer songwriter.'

'Ah,' I said, 'but think Kylie, think Madonna, think J-Lo.'

'What about them?'

'They're all actresses as well as singers. My dad's always saying that working in any part of the media can be feast or famine until you make it big. It's good to have a few strings to your bow. And loads of singers have acted in films as well as pursued their song writing. Come on Iz, it would be another thing that you can offer when you're famous.'

I could see Izzie was thinking about it. One of the things I like about her is that she is into learning about so many things. She's totally open-minded . . . which made me think, I know just how to persuade her . . .

'Thing is, with learning,' I began, 'you can never stop. You can never think that you're there. It's like, you can always improve your performance skills whether it's for stage, singing or acting . . .'

Izzie sighed. 'OK. Enough. You're on. I'm in.'

'Excellent,' I said. 'See Lucy, your mum was right, life never closes a wotsit without opening another wotsit.'

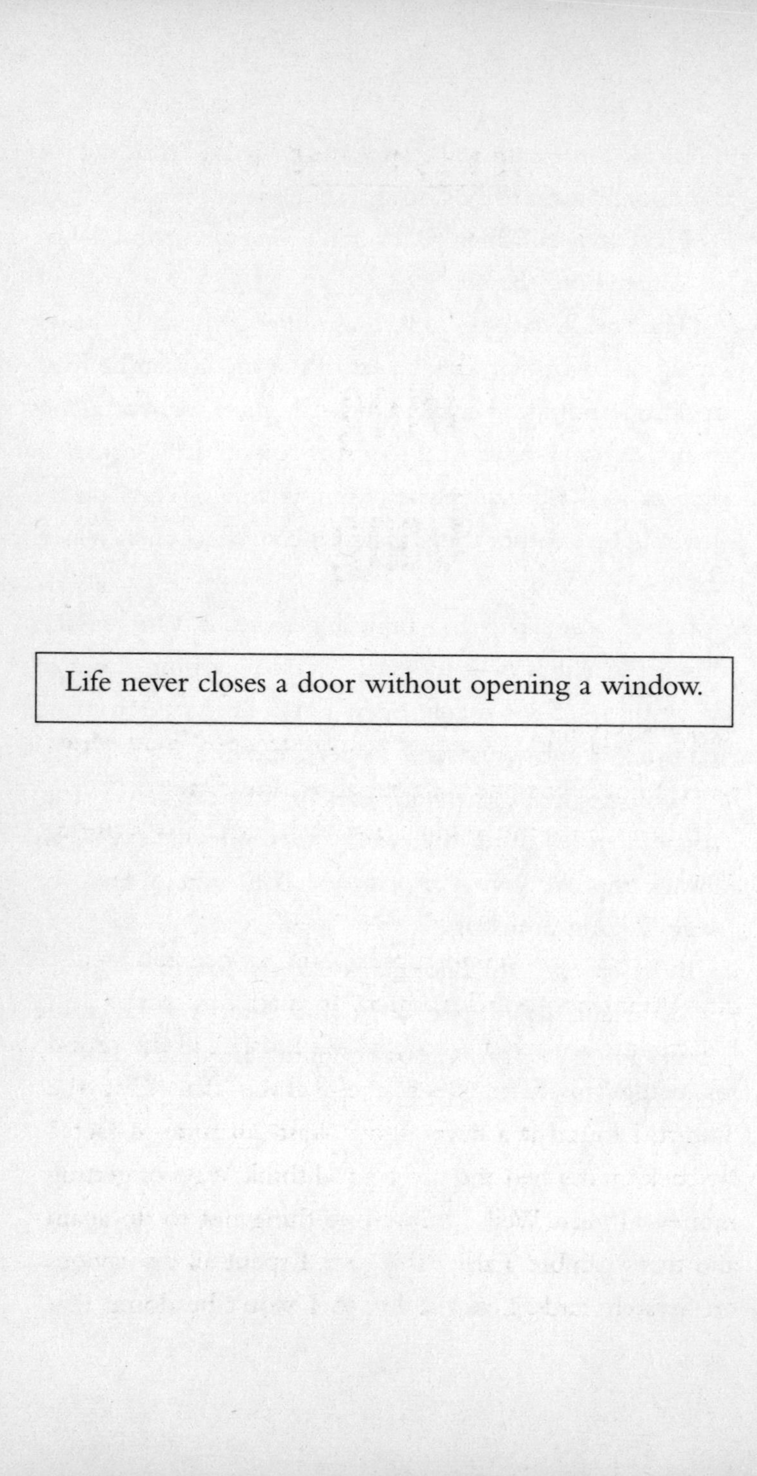

Life never closes a door without opening a window.

Chapter 5

Ding Dong

'Sorry, Nesta love, I thought you understood,' said Mum when I got home and told her about the classes.

'But it's only five pounds for each class. That's pretty good value.'

'I know, but add that up over a term . . .'

'Don't worry,' I interrupted. She looked sad and I didn't want her to feel like that. 'It doesn't matter.'

I went to my room to mope, but I wasn't in the mood for being miserable. Been there, done that. Got the T-shirt. I found it a humongous waste of time in fact. I lay back on my bed and had a good think. Ways of getting money. Hhmm. Well, I know one thing not to do again and that's gamble. Earlier this year, I spent all my savings on Scratch cards. Lost the lot, so I won't be doing that again. No, there must be some job I can do, babysitting or something. Suddenly a light switched on in my head. Course, that's it, I thought as I quickly dialled Lucy's number.

'Hey, Nesta,' said Lucy when she picked up the phone. 'What can I do for you?'

'Actually, Luce, more like what can I do for you? Or more, for your dad that is. Does he need any other workers to do restocking in the shop.'

'He does actually. On Fridays.'

'How much?'

'He pays me five quid an hour. Two hours ten quid.'

'Ask if he'll give me a job.'

I heard Lucy yell at the other end of the phone. 'Dad, can Nesta have a job restocking on Friday nights?'

I heard a distant voice yell back. 'Yes. The more the merrier.'

Lucy came back on the phone. 'Sorted, mate.'

'Excellent. Another string to my bow. Shelf stacker.'

'I'll do some hours with you as well as my Wednesday,' said Lucy. 'Be fun if we're both doing it.'

Ha, I thought as I put the phone down. Where there's a will, there's a way. And it's part of the process according to my dad. He says that loads of great movie stars start out working in dead end jobs, so that they can pay their way before their big break.

★ ★ ★

The following Wednesday, Izzie and I pitched up for our first acting class. It was to be held in Muswell Hill in a place that was an ordinary school in the day time and used for adult education in the evenings.

'That has to be it,' said Izzie as we approached a four storey building. 'It looks like a school with all those windows.'

'And it looks like ours isn't the only night course being held here,' I said. Music was pounding out from every level and we could see girls in leotards ballet dancing on one floor, another bunch jazz dancing on another, others kick-boxing on the ground floor. 'Looks like lots of girls come here, hope there won't be too many boys.'

'Speak for yourself,' said Izzie. 'You may be having a year off boys, but I'm not.'

After signing in at reception, we made our way up to the first floor where our class was to be held. As we waited for the ballet class to finish, a group of people began to assemble outside the door.

Excellent, I thought as I watched them arrive and, like Izzie and me, smile apprehensively at the rest of the group. A bald guy with a beard, a petite white-haired lady, two curly-haired twenty-year-olds, maybe sisters, a chubby guy with glasses, probably in his forties. A couple more middle-aged ladies. Couple more guys, probably in their thirties. Excellent, I thought. Not one cute boy in sight.

Our teacher was a slim red-headed woman in her late twenties called Jo. She started us off with a few introduction games. First we had to say our names and five things about ourselves. I was third.

'Nesta. Star sign Leo. Fave band, Red Hot Chili Peppers. Fave TV programme, *The Simpsons*. Fave food, pizza. Live in Highgate.'

The introductions were a bit of a blur and, by the end of it, I'd only got about four people's names.

Then we had to say our name again and do an action that started with the same letter as your name.

'Make it as mad as you like,' said Jo.

Everyone seemed a bit shy at first, so I decided to start us off as we've done stuff like this in drama at school.

'Nesta. Napping,' I said, then closed my eyes and put my head on one side.

Izzie went next. 'Izzie: itching.' That got a laugh as she played out scratching herself all over. After that the others were off.

'Jan: jumping.'

'Dave: drawing.'

'Catherine: canoeing.'

There were twelve of us in all and the game seemed to do the trick as, afterwards, most of us found we could remember most people's names.

I'm going to enjoy this, I thought as Jo asked us to stand anywhere in the room.

'Choose a character,' she said, 'male or female, any age, then walk round the room as you imagine they would.'

I decided to do a bloke I'd seen walking down Archway Road last week. He walked like a gorilla with a swagger. A real tough man. After we'd swaggered, minced, strode, tiptoed round for a while, Jo asked us to lie on the floor and go to sleep in the manner of our character. I lay in the corner and started snoring. After a while, Jo said, 'OK, now it's six a.m. What's your character doing now?'

I heard a few people get up but I stayed where I was. No way, my character would be out of bed yet. He was a yob. Probably didn't even know that there were two six o'clocks in a day.

Jo went on. 'And now it's seven a.m.' I could hear more people get up. When she said, 'Eight,' even more got up. As she said, 'Nine,' then, 'Ten,' then, 'Eleven. What's your character doing now?' I could hear that everyone was up. I opened my eyes and sneaked a look. My fellow luvvies were acting their socks off, miming driving, typing, on the phone, eating, talking, having a life.

'OK, twelve o'clock and what are your characters doing now?' said Jo. 'Er, on the floor, Napping Nesta isn't it? Is there a problem? I see your character hasn't done anything? Are you stuck about what to do?'

'Oh no,' I said. 'My character's a lazy yob and never gets out of bed before one.'

In the corner, Izzie cracked up.

'OK,' said Jo. 'Maybe your yob could get up a bit earlier today so that you get something out of the exercise.'

'OK,' I said. I got up, mimed having a fag, lay about, scratched a bit, watched telly and studied the others. Some people were really going for it. Bet they're sorry they picked such overactive characters, I thought as I mimed having another fag.

When we'd all finished our day, everyone had to say what character they'd been doing. Izzie, poor thing, had played her mum and had had to get up at six-thirty to go to work. She had her mum's walk down really well though.

'People think that acting is about learning lines,' said Jo, 'and to some degree of course, it is. But there's so much more to it than that, which is why I wanted to start with this exercise. Think about it. Before someone has even opened their mouth, other people have made an assessment or a judgement. Why is it, we steer away from certain people on the street, others we feel are OK?'

'Clothes, image,' I said. 'Your choice of style says a lot about you.'

'Yes, but even more than that,' said Jo. 'Any ideas?'

'Body language,' said Jan, the white-haired lady.

'Exactly,' said Jo. 'How people walk, how they sit, how they hold themselves, says infinitely more than what they choose to verbalise or choose to wear. In the same way, if you want to act, your audience has to know who your character is the second you walk on the stage, way before you begin to say your lines. It's not enough to just put on a costume. You can't just walk on as you in another person's clothes and expect to be believed as someone else.'

What Jo said was very true, I thought. One of the things I love doing is sitting in cafés watching people go by and I've always thought that you can tell so much about them by how they walk, whether they scrunch their shoulders up, if they stride or dawdle. Like even at school, without visuals, you can tell which teacher is coming along the corridor by the sound of their footsteps. Mrs Allen's are really quick, confident, like she doesn't have time to waste. Click, clack, click. Miss Watkins' are slower, more considered, sort of ploddy, like she is. I'm going to really watch people and how they walk from now on, I decided, so that I can put it into practice for different roles in my acting career.

After the 'character' exercise, we played some games where we had to close our eyes and wander round the room trying to work out where other people were by the sounds they made. At first I couldn't see the point of it, but afterwards Jo explained that one of the first things you had to learn on stage was awareness of other actors. 'So many people are so concerned about doing their bit, their moment in the spotlight, that they forget that they're part of a team.'

By the end of the class, I was well impressed. I felt I'd learned loads in just over an hour and still had much, much more to discover.

'That was five quid well spent,' I whispered to Izzie as we got our coats to leave at the end. She nodded and, as I turned to the windowsill to get my scarf, I was aware that someone had walked in behind us.

Izzie nudged me. 'Eyes left,' she said. 'Ding *do-nnggg*.'

Ding dong is our new alert for when there's talent around. Lucy's brother Lal started it after he'd watched the movie, *Carry On Nurse*. Leslie Phillips plays a character called Jack Bell in the film and he says, 'Ding dong' whenever he sees someone he fancies. We've all started saying it now along with, 'Oo, matron!', an expression used by the character played by Kenneth Williams in later *Carry On* films. People at school think we're mad, but we all think it's hysterically funny especially if Mrs Allen is reading out something really serious and Lucy, TJ, Izzie and I all turn to each other and mouth, 'Oo, matron!'

I turned to see a boy going up to Jo. I couldn't see his face, but from the back he had dark hair and was wearing a calf-length tweedy coat and a red scarf. Trained up as I was now, I could tell just by his body language that he was flustered. Izzie and I strained to hear what he was saying.

'I'm *so* sorry,' he said. 'I went to the wrong place. I thought the class was at the Institute so I went there then by the time I discovered I was in the wrong place, the class here had already started. I tried to get here, but I had to wait ages for a bus and . . .'

Jo smiled at him. 'No problem. At least now you know where we are for next week.' She checked her list. 'You must be . . . Luke.'

'Yeah. Luke De Biasi.'

'Well, it's a bit late to introduce you now,' said Jo indicating the rest of us, 'as we're all just leaving, but these are the people who will be in the class with you.'

As Luke turned round to look at the group, I quickly turned away, so that he wouldn't catch me staring. Izzie wasn't as cool. She dug her elbow into my back and whispered, 'Hubba hubba.'

I couldn't resist, so turned for a quick peek at him. When I saw his face, my peek became a look that lasted . . . and lasted . . . I couldn't help it. I knew that I ought to look away, but something in his eyes held me like a magnet. Time slowed down and my heart seemed to speed up. It was like Luke and I were the only two people in the room. Finally I broke his gaze and ran.

Ding *dong*: – talent in the vicinity.

Hubba bubba: – cor! He's tasty.

Oo, matron!: – oo, *er*!

Chapter 6

Oo, Matron!

Aghhhhhhhhhhhhhhhhhh. Uggggggggg. *Arghhhhhhhhhh.* That's all I can say, I thought, as I stared at my reflection in the wardrobe mirror before I got into bed later that night. Sometimes life is so unfair. Why, oh *why* would I have to see the boy of my dreams when I look like a tin opener? We haven't even met properly. We haven't *even* spoken and yet I know that he's special. I felt like I'd seen him before, then I remembered where. TJ's house. There's a painting in their hall. TJ said it's by a Pre-Raphaelite painter called Edward Burne-Jones and it's called 'The Tree of Forgiveness'. Anyway, Luke looks like the man in it. Dark eyes, high cheek bones, wide mouth and I loved the coat he wore to the drama class. It looked like vintage American, like the ones that men wore in old black and white movie classics. Really cool. I smiled at my reflection again. The killer shark from the film *Jaws* grimaced back at me. No. There was no getting away from it. I looked horrible. The girls may say I have other things going for me but, when I open my mouth, all you see is the brace. It's like, you can have a huge fifty foot white wall but, if there's one black dot on it, that's what your eye will be drawn towards. So agh. Ug. Argh. And, as Izzie would say, poo.

Luke. I could still see him in my mind's eye. Aristocratic-looking. Roman-looking in fact. His name is Italian. Luke De Biasi. Probably called Luca at home. He was very good-looking, but more than that, and I know Izzie would laugh at me for saying it, he looked intelligent. He did. There was something in his eyes. And I don't mean contact lenses.

Anyway that's the last time I'll see him, I thought, because no way can I go back to that class if he's going to be in it. I'll have to wait a year and bump into him when I've had my brace off and can smile at people and talk to them again.

Izzie said I was being stupid when I told her that I wasn't going back. Honestly, and she has the cheek to say that I'm blunt sometimes. Calling me stupid. Huh! That's not exactly tact city. She doesn't understand. I could never relax in class knowing that he was there, watching me, thinking nice face, shame about the metal munchers. No,

I couldn't possibly. I know that boys imagine snogging as well as girls, but I can't believe that braces figure highly on the fave fantasy girl requirement list. Like: nice hair, good legs, great bod, attractive mouth, brace.

I don't know. Maybe I *could* go back to class. I could be a quiet member of the group. An observer. There to learn. I could be silent. Never open my mouth. I could be mysterious. Enigmatic.

Hah! Who am I kidding? Gobby is my middle name.

I spent a few minutes practising my closed mouth smile in the mirror as I considered my options.

Forget him? Not an option.

Postpone meeting him until the brace is removed? No. Can't do that. He might have a girlfriend by then. Yikes. He might have a girlfriend *now*! Of course he might. Probably does. All the more reason for *not* postponing meeting him. I have to find out where I stand.

Go to class but disguise the fact I have a brace in. Hhhmm. Maybe. Yes. I think that's the best plan. Is it? Isn't it? I know! I could get one of those head-to-toe tent dresses that some Muslim women wear to cover themselves. I could pretend I'm a new girl in class and I *am* Muslim. Yes! That's it. No one would ever know. Izzie could just say that Nesta decided not to do the class any more, but another friend of hers has come instead. Her *Muslim* friend, Mustapha Bracein. Then I could watch him from inside my dress. Burkas, I think they're called.

Yeah. Brilliant idea. Or is it? Hhmm. Best sleep on it, I thought, I can't decide now and if I try to, I think I may well blow a fuse in my brain.

I woke up the next morning with the solution. Or solutions. Disguise, distraction and decoys. My first plan was to wear a balaclava not a burka. Tony's got one for when he eventually gets to go skiing. He is funny. He knows Mum hasn't got the money to pay for him to go and he hasn't got any of the really expensive equipment he needs, but he has got a balaclava. Izzie told him that he had to start somewhere and that sometimes if you make a symbolic step towards your goal/dream or whatever, the universe conspires to make it happen. Yeah, right. Mystic Izzie. She's bonkers. Anyway, Tony let me borrow his strange but symbolic woolly hat, but sadly it didn't go down too well at school.

'Nesta Williams, can you give me any explanation as to why you find it necessary to wear a woolly hat in the art class?' asked Mrs Elwes.

'It's a balaclava, Miss.'

'I don't care what it is. You're not wearing it in my class.'

'Yes, Miss.'

My next tactic didn't go down too well either.

'And what period are we studying in history at the moment, Nesta?' asked Miss Watkins.

'Tudors, Miss.'

'Not the Egyptians?'

'No, Miss.'

'Then perhaps you could explain why you have a scarf wrapped around your neck and face in the manner of an Egyptian mummy.'

'I'm cold, Miss.'

'So get a thermal vest, girl. In the meantime, take off the scarf. I like to be able to see the faces of my pupils when I'm teaching. To make sure that they're still awake.'

Lucy thought it was hysterical. 'You in a thermal vest,' she said as we made our way out of school in the afternoon. 'That I'd like to see.'

'No *way*. So uncool,' I said.

'Thermal vest, so uncool. Course they are, that's why they're thermal. Oh very good, Nesta,' said Lucy laughing her head off. Sometimes I think she takes too many vitamins or something. It seems that all my friends are mad. Apart from TJ maybe, but give it time.

'So what's with all the headgear today?' asked TJ.

'I'm trying a few things out before the next acting class,' I said. 'To disguise my brace.' Of course, I'd filled TJ and Lucy in on meeting Luke as soon as I'd got home last night. They were very sympathetic, but both of them thought I should go back to the class and not consider giving it up for a moment.

'If this guy is worth bothering about,' said TJ, 'he's not

going to be put off by your brace. I think you should be brave. Be who and what you are and if he doesn't like it, forget him.'

'I guess you're right on one level,' I said. 'But on another level, boys are highly visual. They go on what they see and if they like it. The time for being who you are, hairy legs, strange habits, brace or whatever, comes later. First you have to lure them in . . . You know that, TJ.'

TJ sighed and nodded. At the end of Year Nine, she had a crush on a boy who lived next door to her. Only problem was that he saw her as one of the lads, a mate, so she had to seriously reconsider her image and get him to see her as a girl. It worked too except, once he was interested, she realised that he was *really* boring.

'Yeah,' said TJ. 'I think it's sad but true. Boys do like girls who look like girls.'

'Exactly,' I said. And then I had my most brilliant idea.

Half an hour later, we were in the lingerie department of a store at the Mall.

'And are you going to explain why having a brace put in has resulted in a strange compulsion to buy underwear?' asked Lucy.

'Distraction,' I said. 'Obvious isn't it?'

'Yes, shopping is always a good distraction . . .'

'Not for *us.* For boys,' I explained. 'See, it was when TJ said that boys like girls who look like girls that I realised, that's what I have to do. Get boys distracted from my face and the way to do that is . . .' I indicated the racks of gorgeous girlie underwear.

'Show them your knickers?' asked Lucy.

'*No*.'

Lucy laughed. 'Wear your knickers on your head? That would cover your brace.'

'*Noooo*. Don't be mad. I mean, show them my chesty bits. Have you ever been with a boy when you're showing even the tiniest bit of cleavage?'

'The *tiniest* bit of cleavage is sadly all I've got,' sighed Lucy as she eyed the rails.

Izzie nodded. 'Yeah, it's like their eyes are pulled towards it by some magnetic force. They can't help it. When I wore a low top to band rehearsal one evening, it was hysterical. The boys were doing their best not to look, but I could see their cheeks starting to twitch with the effort. Biff didn't even try not to look. He just talked to my chest all night.'

'I hate that,' said TJ. 'It's like you're a walking pair of boobs and nothing else.'

Lucy grinned. 'You know that song by Frank Sinatra's daughter Nancy, "These Boots Are Made For Walking"? We ought to sing, "These Boobs Are Made For Walking".'

TJ patted her on the head. 'Keep taking the tablets, Lucy,' she said.

'Boys can't help it,' I said. 'It's their hormones. I know

sometimes it's horrible being leered at, but it can be used to your advantage. Like my next meeting with Luke. My plan is to buy the most uplifting fab-shaped bra there is in this shop then wear it, so that he will be so busy looking at my marvellous chest that he won't notice that my mouth is full of metal.'

'He's going to look up sometime, Nesta,' said TJ.

'And when he does, I'll shut my mouth. I'll only talk when he's looking at my cleavage.'

'You're bonkers,' laughed Izzie.

No, I'm not. It's simple, I thought. That is until we started to look for the bra. After fifteen minutes I was totally confused. There were rails and rails of them. Not just colours and fabrics but types: bras for total support, egoboosters, minimisers, bras with no front, no back, balcony bras, wired, plunge, moulded, padded, seamed, non-padded, five-way, sheer, strapless, halter-neck, crossover, one-shoulder, bioform, sculptured, push up, multiway, T-shirt, sports, stretch cup. They even had thermal ones.

'Arghhhhhh,' I cried. 'I've seen Hitchcock's film, *The Birds*. But now showing at a store near you. *The Bras*. They're mean, they're keen, they're taking over.'

TJ, Izzie and Lucy cracked up laughing as I swung five bras up in the air and made them fly like birds.

A shop assistant gave me a funny look, so I put the bras back on the rails. 'But how are you supposed to know which one is best?' I asked. 'Do I need a bioform or a five-way push up?'

'I would imagine five-way push ups are for aliens,' said Lucy. 'As they are the only beings who could possibly have five boobs to push up.'

This time it was Izzie who patted her on the head. 'Poor dear,' she said. 'We really ought not to let you out again.'

TJ pointed at a notice on the wall and began to laugh. 'God. Have you seen this?'

We gathered round to read the notice. 'How to calculate your bra size,' it said.

'First you need a degree in maths,' said TJ. 'Measure your ribcage, add four for an even number, five for an odd number. Measure your full bust then subtract the bra size from the full size to give you your cup size.'

There was a tape measure on the wall next to the notice.

TJ got out her calculator. 'You measure and I'll calculate,' she said.

Lucy got out some paper and wrote as I measured my ribcage then round my bust. 'Why are bras sold in inches when the rest of the world has gone metric?' she asked.

'Dunno,' I said. 'But all I wanted was to buy a bra. Not do an engineering class.'

TJ ignored me. 'Thirty-two B,' she said after a few moments. 'Easy.'

'Yeah. That's what my mum always gets me and her method is very scientific. She guesses it. Easy.'

We picked out a few bras, but in the end decided that the 'egobooster' looked like it might give the best cleavage effect. I picked one from the rails, took it into the dressing room and tried it on.

'Oo, matron!' the girls chorused as they stuck their heads round the curtain five minutes later.

'Too much?' I asked as I took in my reflection.

'You could get a leading role in *Lethal Weapon 2*,' said TJ laughing.

'Only it would be called *Lethal Weapons, I Have Two*,' said Lucy.

'Well I think it will definitely distract him,' said Izzie, 'but it might be a bit obvious turning up to class in that when the majority of the other people are middle-aged and dressed in baggy tracksuits.'

I sighed. 'So what next?' I asked. 'I've tried headgear. Bras. Scarves.'

'You could pretend that you're dumb,' said TJ.

'*Brilliant* idea!' I said. 'I could learn sign language.'

TJ looked taken aback. 'I was joking,' she said.

'Anyway, the rest of the class know you can speak from last week,' said Izzie.

I felt miserable. All my good ideas had come to nothing. I would just have to talk with my hand over my mouth or perfect the art of talking through closed lips.

Nope. Even I knew that no way was I going to be able to do that in an acting class. No. It was too sad, but I would have to resort back to option B. Oh cruel world, I thought. I would have to let Luke go and not go back to the class at all. True love was not meant to be mine. I would just have to grow old with my memories of how it could have been. On the other hand, it would make me more beautiful as people would be able to sense my loss, the sadness behind the smiles, the inner wistfulness behind the mask of success. Yes, mine would be a high but lonely destiny.

I sniffed and tried to look noble. 'It happens in all the best movies you know? In *Dr Zhivago*, after many years apart, he sees Lara, the love of his life, at the end. He jumps off a bus to try and catch her but, too late, he has a heart attack and dies on the pavement and she never knows how close he was. And in *Wuthering Heights*, Cathy dies leaving her one true love, Heathcliff, heartbroken forever. Sometimes it's not meant to be . . .'

Izzie raised her eyes to the ceiling. 'Oh for Gawd's sake. Nesta. Luvvie. Dwarling. You've got a *brace*, not a noose around your neck. You are not dead. Luke is not dead. Life is not over.'

'You don't understand the pain of unrequited love,' I said through closed lips. 'Or true passion.'

Izzie turned and grinned at TJ and Lucy. 'True passion? Oh yes I do. And two words sum it up. Chocolate fudge.'

'Yeah, bugger unrequited love and passion,' said Lucy. 'Chocolate never lets you down. And it doesn't care what your teeth look like. Come on. Food department. Now.'

'Best idea you've had all day,' said TJ and the three of them headed off for the chocolate counters like homing pigeons. Huh, I thought as I watched them charge off. Am I misunderstood or what? But what can you do? I thought as I hurried to catch them up. If you can't beat them, join them.

How to Measure for a Bra

1) Measure in inches around the ribcage directly under your boobs.
2) If it's an odd number, add 5 inches, if it's an even number, add 4 inches.
3) This gives you your bra size (e.g., 31 inches + 5 inches = 36 inches, or 34 inches + 4 inches = 38 inches)
4) Then measure the fullest part of your bust. The difference between the full bust measurement and the bra size measurement gives you your cup size. For instance:

1 inch smaller than bra size = AA-cup size
Same as bra size = A-cup
1 inch bigger than bra size = B-cup
2 inch bigger than bra size = C-cup
3 inch bigger than bra size = D-cup
4 inch bigger than bra size = DD-cup
5 inch bigger than bra size = E-cup
6 inch bigger than bra size = F-cup
7 inch bigger than bra size = G cup
and any bigger that that, you need an over-the-shoulder boulder holder, not a bra.

Note from Nesta: *Whadttttt*? Forget all that. Most large department stores offer a professional measuring service for bra sizes for free. Sounds good to me.

Chapter 7

Wahey and Hurrahalot

Life is full of surprises.

My brother Tony takes girl chasing seriously. *Very* seriously. Girls are his favourite hobby and he likes to think of himself as the Casanova of North London. The pro. The Master. He who knows about girls. Part of me thinks that it's hysterical as I live with him. I've seen him in the morning when he's just woken up (not a pretty sight). I've seen him when he's been ill and wants his mum (also not a pretty sight). But another part of me has to hand it to him. His dedication to his art does seem to pay off and there's always a queue of girls desperate for his attention. Part of his girl chasing degree has been researching the perfect place to take a girl for a romantic evening. And he thinks he's found it.

‘I read a review in the local paper,’ he said. ‘Family run restaurant, intimate, unpretentious, slightly bohemian, fab food and not too expensive. Voted the area’s favourite restaurant by locals for five years running.’

‘And?’

‘I need you to come and give me your opinion before I book it for . . .’

‘You and Lucy?’

He nodded. ‘Yeah, if she’ll come.’

‘Sure.’

So there I was on Friday evening waiting in a restaurant for my brother who, as usual, was late. I didn’t mind too much though as I’d spent the last hour stacking shelves at Lucy’s dad’s shop and it was good to sit down and relax. Quite a funky-looking place, I thought as I scraped some wax off the wine bottle that served as a candle holder in front of me. There were red and white gingham cloths on the tables and the walls were a colourful mishmash of amateur paintings, faded photos of people from times gone by, postcards from all over the world. All were fighting for space and none were winning.

‘Would you like to order?’ said a voice to my right.

‘Um. I’m waiting for someone,’ I said looking up. When I saw who it was, I clapped my hand over my mouth. ‘*You*!’

It was Luke. Even in his waiter’s apron, he looked Pre-Raphaelite and gorgeous.

He laughed and placed a basket of bread and a small bowl of olive oil in front of me. 'Yeah. It's me. Why? What did I do?'

'Oh, nothing,' I said from behind my hand. 'Just . . . you're the guy from class the other night. What are you doing here?'

'I work here two nights a week. What's your excuse?'

'Waiting for my brother.'

Ohmigod, ohmigod, ohmigod, I thought, as my heart started thumping in my chest. This is what Iz is always on about. Fate. Just as I'd decided to be all tragic and never see Luke again, destiny decides otherwise. Wahey and hurrahalot. Let's hear it for destiny.

'OK,' he said getting out his note-pad. 'So what would you like while you're waiting?'

I suppose a snog's out of the question, I thought before I could stop myself. I almost blushed then told myself, no relax, Nesta. He can't read your mind.

'Appuchino,' I muttered.

'Pardon?'

'Carperino.'

'Sorry, I can't understand what you're saying. Your hand seems to be superglued to your top lip . . .'

I put my hand down and attempted to speak without opening my mouth. 'Uepurino,' I said.

Luke looked knowingly at me. 'Brace, huh?' he said gently.

Uh? Am I *that* obvious? 'No. Yeah. How did you know?'

Luke pointed behind him to a very pretty dark-haired girl behind the counter. 'Marisa. She had one until last month. She did the same. Hid behind her hand.'

My heart sank. She was gorgeous. Obviously his girlfriend as she smiled when he turned to look at her.

'So she works here too?'

Luke nodded. 'It's our dad's restaurant . . .'

His *sister*?! Yabadabadoo.

'It's well worth it, you know,' continued Luke.

'Owning a restaurant?'

'*No*. Having a brace.' He called Marisa over. 'Hey. Marisa, this is . . . I don't know your name.'

'Nesta,' I said from behind my hand.

'Brace,' said Marisa.

I nodded.

'Just in?'

I nodded again. 'Week almost.'

She gave me a huge smile revealing perfect teeth. 'It's worth it in the end, but it's awful when it first goes in. Feels like everyone's looking at you.'

I nodded.

'People don't even notice,' said Luke. 'I never really noticed Marisa's. I think she was more conscious of it than anyone.'

'So how do you two know each other?' asked Marisa.

Luke looked around as though looking for someone then whispered, 'We're doing the same course.'

'Why the secrecy?' I whispered back.

'You tell her,' said Marisa. 'What do you want, Nesta?'

'Cappuccino, thanks,' I said.

Luke turned to go, but Marisa pulled him back. 'No, Luca, you sit, it's quiet. Explain.'

After she'd disappeared, Luke sat opposite me. As soon as he looked into my eyes, I felt myself getting hot and my insides felt like they were melting. He was amazing looking. Sooooooo beautiful. I hadn't imagined it. It's a weird thing that when I first meet someone, I can remember what they look like for about a day, then it fades, like from sharp focus to blurry. Seeing him again was a real blast back to picture perfect.

Luke looked down at the table. 'I'm supposed to be doing an accountancy course.'

'Oh . . . and?'

'On *Wednesday* nights . . .'

'Ah.' Oh well done on the brilliant conversation, Nesta, I thought. Oh. And. Ah. Yes, riveting stuff. Luckily, he didn't seem to notice.

'Yeah. Ah,' continued Luke. 'Dad's in the restaurant business. He has three now. This one which has been here for years, one in Soho and he's just opened a third up near Harrow, not far from where I go to school actually. It's quite handy for popping into at lunch-time. Anyway, my brother runs the Soho restaurant and Dad wants me to be involved when I leave school after my A-levels, maybe oversee the Harrow one. I want to act. It's all I've ever wanted to do but he's dead against it. So . . . I told him I was going to do accountancy to help with the business when, in fact, I'm doing acting. That's why I was late last week. Dad dropped me off at the accountancy course and I had to dash like mad to get to the acting.'

'But what will happen if he drops you every week? You'll never make it.'

'It was just last week. My car was being serviced, but I've got it back now and can drive myself.'

Hhmm. Is gorgeous *and* has own car, I thought. Not that I am influenced by things like that at all. Not at *all*. I am *deep* and *beyond* material trappings. But . . . hhmm . . . I wonder what kind of car?

'But . . . what are you going to do at the end of the course when you haven't learned anything about figures?'

Luke laughed. 'I shall act dumb. By then, I should have the skills.' Then he shrugged. 'Dunno. I'll think of something.'

After that, we chatted for a while about acting and films and which he liked and which he hated. As we talked I realised that he knew a lot about them. He mentioned films I'd never heard of and he seemed to know who had directed them and who had produced them. As I listened to him, I began to feel out of my depth, because I watch films just for fun. That awful feeling that I might be shallow and boring came creeping back and I resolved to swot up on who was who and what was what in the film industry. Hhhmm, how can I impress you without revealing that I don't know half as much about films as you do, I wondered as I stared at his bottom lip and tried to commit it to memory.

Suddenly what to say was obvious.

'My dad's a director,' I blurted out.

'Really? Wow!' said Luke. 'Lucky you. Films, TV or documentary?'

'TV mostly. Dramas. But I think he'd like to do a film, you know, for the big screen.'

Luke nodded. 'Must be amazing. And there was me rabbiting on about films when you're the real expert with your dad in the biz.'

Yeah, right. Me the expert, I thought as I gave him my lips-closed smile.

'I wish my father did something interesting,' continued Luke. 'I can't tell you how much I don't want to be involved in his restaurant business.'

'But involved how? What does he want you to be? Chef? Manager?'

'Bit of both. That's how it is in a family business.'

I couldn't resist. I stuffed two big bits of bread in front of my teeth in my lower cheeks then attempted my impersonation of Marlon Brando as he was in *The*

Godfather. 'So, Luca, de family needs you,' I drawled in an Italian accent.

He laughed. 'Excellent,' he said. 'Marlon Brando. *The Godfather*?'

I nodded and desperately tried to swallow the bread, praying that it hadn't got caught in my brace. How attractive would that be? Not. I put my hand back over my mouth just in case.

'Can you cook?' I asked.

'I'm Italian. Course I can.'

'I'm half Italian,' I said. 'I can half cook.' Actually that's a lie, I can't cook to save my life, but it made him laugh.

'So you know what it's like then. Life revolves round the kitchen.'

'Er, yeah. Round the kitchen. Curries, pasta, you name it,' I said. 'I can produce a great meal at the drop of a hat.' Not a complete lie, I thought. All it takes is a quick phone call to the takeaway place and hey presto, *voilà*, il supperoni.

Just at that moment, Tony came in so I introduced them along with my quick explanation as to why we look so different. 'Same dad, different mothers,' I said. 'Dad's where we get the Italian genes from.'

'And she doesn't mean Armani jeans,' smiled Tony, then started laughing at his own joke.

Luke slid out of his seat to let him sit down. 'And the gift of cooking, I hear,' he said.

Tony looked at me quizzically.

'Well, no. Mum can cook as well,' I said. 'She's from Jamaica and does a mean curry.'

'Sounds good,' said Luke turning to Tony. 'Your sister was just telling me what a great cook she is.'

Tony looked surprised. 'She *was*?' I could see that he was about to laugh, but I kicked him under the table and he straightened his face. 'I mean. Yeah. She is. Always cooking stuff up is our Nesta.'

Another customer caught Luke's eye. 'Won't be a mo,' he said as he went to take the man's order.

'So what do you think?' asked Tony looking round after he'd gone. 'Romantic or what? Do you think Lucy will like it?'

'She'll feel very at home here. It's kind of a cosy mess, just like the kitchen at her house.' I looked over at Luke and sighed. 'And it is possibly the most romantic place I've ever been in my whole life . . .'

Tony glanced over at Luke. 'Ah. The waiter. That was quick.'

'Luca De Biasi,' I said. 'His dad owns the restaurant. He's doing the acting course I'm doing . . .'

Tony nodded. 'Ah, he's the guy you fell in love with on Wednesday . . .'

I nodded back. 'Fate has given me a second chance.'

'And maybe she'll even give you a third.' Tony smiled mischievously as Luke came back and handed us menus.

'The lasagne is good tonight,' said Luke.

Tony glanced at the menu. 'Hey, Nesta,' he said. 'Why don't you invite Luke to come and try your *unbelievable* cookery skills.'

Whadtt!! I thought, no way. But Luke was looking at me to see my reaction and I didn't want him to feel that I didn't want to see him again. Arrghhh. What to do? Um. I know! Agree to it but don't give a date. Be vague and hopefully he'll forget about it.

'Yeah sure,' I said. 'I'd love to cook for you sometime, Luke.'

'Mum and Dad are out tomorrow night,' Tony said with a grin. 'If you're not busy, would you like to come over then?'

'Yeah. Cool,' said Luke. 'I look forward to it.'

Tony sniggered. 'Yeah. And I can assure you that it will be an experience you'll never forget.'

Tony Costello, you are dead, I thought as I kicked him again under the table.

Tony's Top Romantic Places

- Anywhere candlelit.
- Biasi's Italian restaurant.
- Kenwood on Hampstead Heath on a hot summer's night when there's a concert on.
- Back seat of the movies (still a good one, particularly if it's a horror movie as the girl will need to hold your hand).
- Any funky café with big old sofas to sink into.
- Tony's bedroom.

Note from Nesta: this last one only works for Tony . . .

Chapter 8

Recipe for Disaster

Move over Nigella, there's a new domestic goddess in town I thought as I lay in a jasmine-scented bath the following evening. Everything was sorted. The table was laid. My chicken curry was cooking nicely in the oven. Mum and Dad were out of the way until after their movie finished. My guests would be arriving in half an hour. (I'd phoned Lucy and begged her to come and join us, so that it wasn't Luke and me with Tony sitting in the middle having a right laugh.) All I had left to do was light the candles. This entertaining lark is easy peasy, I thought as I lathered my legs with Mum's Guerlain bath gel.

'Keep it simple,' Mum'd advised earlier. 'You don't want to be in a panic when your guests arrive, so do something you can prepare beforehand and just warm it up when people arrive.'

She'd been fab and offered to help when I told her of my dilemma. Between the two of us, we'd made a Jamaican curry, my grandmother's recipe. I thought Luke'd like something different from the Italian meals he must get every night.

'All you have to do is turn on the oven,' said Mum before she'd left. 'A hundred and eighty degrees centigrade for an hour and twenty minutes.'

After my bath, I got changed into my black halter-neck top and black jeans, put on my make-up then lit the candles.

By the time Luke arrived, the flat looked warm and inviting.

'Wow, this is nice,' he said as I gave him a quick guided tour. I have to hand it to Mum, I thought, as we went from room to room, she really does know how to create a comfortable atmosphere with her use of warm colours, Moroccan rugs and Eastern artefacts. Luke particularly liked looking at Dad's black and white photos that lined the hall walls. And he spent ages looking at Dad's film books on the bookshelf in the sitting room. I made a mental note to have a look at some of them myself as the doorbell rang and I went to let Lucy in.

I felt so grown-up. Like I was playing the part of a hostess at an adult dinner party in a movie. Lucy was a bit shy when she first arrived, as she's not used to having proper dinner here with candles and the big table in the sitting room set and everything. Usually it's a slice of pizza on the knees in front of the telly. She soon relaxed though and I could tell she liked Luke because, when he went to look at our CDs, she did a fake swoon with her hand on her heart then gave me the thumbs up.

I looked at my watch as Luke put my new chill out CD on. 'Supper should be ready,' I said as I showed everyone where to sit at the table.

When I went into the kitchen to get the curry out of the oven, something didn't feel right. Or should I say, smell right. Whenever Mum cooked it, you could smell the spices and garlic wafting out of the oven long before it was ready. I couldn't smell anything. I lifted the dish from the oven. Oh *noooooo*. Cold. It was stone cold. Uncooked. Raw.

'Need a hand?' asked Tony coming up behind me.

'More than a hand. Blooming oven's not working.'

Tony bent over, looked at the oven then laughed. 'It's not broken Nesta. You turned the grill on but not the oven.'

I looked at the switches. The grill symbol was just above the oven symbol. 'Oh *no*! Oh *no*.' I hated things like this happening. Mum had got this posh new oven last year and using it was *really* complicated. It could do all sorts of things if you knew how to work it. It probably even turned into a private plane if you knew what knobs to turn, but I hadn't got the hang of it. I hate reading all those techno manuals that assume that the reader is fluent in domestic appliance speak. Why couldn't it just have an on/off button then simpletons like me could use it.

Tony laughed again and pointed at the dials. 'You have to turn it on. To oven, not grill, and then you have to put it to the temperature you want.'

'Oh don't laugh. What are we going to do?'

'What do you want to do?'

'Dunno. Crawl away and hide. I mean, how's it going to look? I'll be a laughing stock. He'll think, Nesta. Cook? Why she can't even turn the cooker on. Pathetic. He'll think I'm soooo pathetic.'

'We could heat it up now,' suggested Tony.

'Takes an hour and a half,' I said. 'They'll be starving.' I felt like crying. I wanted it all to be so perfect and now it was ruined.

'Can I take anything through?' asked Luke appearing at the kitchen door.

I was about to blurt out that I was a complete idiot and he may as well go home and give up on me right there and then, when Tony pulled on my arm.

'Um, bit of a problem, mate,' he said. 'Fuse has blown on the cooker I think. No heat.'

Oh, bless him, I thought. He can be a real pal when he wants. I made a mental note to back him up in some way when he needed my support in the future.

'Want me to take a look?' asked Luke. 'I'm fixing stuff all the time at the restaurant.'

'Noo*oooo*,' said Tony. 'Best not mess with it. It can be a bit dodgy sometimes. No. We thought we'd . . .'

'Get take-out,' I interrupted, then I remembered Tony and I didn't have much money between us. Oh God, what to do now? It would be rude to ask our guests to pay for their own meals after we'd invited them.

Tony had obviously realised the same thing. He squeezed my arm again. 'No. We don't need to do take-away. We're Italian,' he said. 'So . . . We've er . . . got the microwave. I'm sure we can knock something up.'

He started opening cupboards and pulling out pots and jars. Our evening is turning into a disaster, I thought. Tony's like me and he can't even boil an egg without ruining it.

'Does the top part of the cooker still work?' asked Luke.

Tony switched one of the switches. 'Yeah. The hob is gas, it's only the oven that's electric.'

'Got any pasta?' asked Luke.

Tony nodded.

'Parmesan cheese?'

Tony nodded again.

'Nesta. You've done your bit for the night. You go and join Lucy and I'll knock us something up,' said Luke. 'Give us a hand, Tony?'

Tony nodded, so I went into the sitting room to join Lucy.

'Oh, poor you,' she said, after I'd told her what had happened. 'But hey, a boy who can cook, looks like a Roman god and seems genuinely nice.'

'I know. I think he may be out of my league,' I said.

Lucy's jaw fell open. 'Out of your league? In all the time I've known you, I have never heard you say anything so ridiculous.'

I was feeling miserable. 'I think he is. Like, he is gorgeous, but more than that, he seems to be good at everything. Bright. He's soon going to find out that I'm a total airhead. In fact that's what he must be thinking now. I bet he's worked out what happened and that I can't even work the cooker. God, I'm soooo stupid.'

'Rubbish,' said Lucy. 'I don't know what's got into you lately. You're not stupid and he wouldn't be here if he didn't like you. I bet he's grilling Tony about you right now and trying to find out all he can about you.' Then she laughed. 'Geddit? Grilling Tony. Luke's a chef. Grilling Tony? Hope not. Cannibalism isn't my thing.'

I gave her my Queen Victoria, 'We are not amused' look.

'Sorry,' she said. 'Couldn't resist. But I bet he is trying to find out more about you.'

'Do you think? Let's go and listen.'

We sneaked into the hall and eavesdropped on the

boys. They seemed to be getting on brilliantly. Chatting away about cars. Tony was telling Luke about Dad refusing to let him have driving lessons.

I had to laugh at them when I poked my head round the door. They looked so domesticated. Luke in Mum's Marge Simpson apron and Tony chopping tomatoes.

'You should have your own TV show,' I said. 'Move over Jamie Oliver, Luke and Tony have come to town.'

Half an hour later, Luke brought in a big bowl of pasta. It was absolutely perfect and tasted amazing. Lucy even helped herself to an extra bowlful. Tony chatted away happily, but I didn't say very much as I was still feeling like an idiot because of the cooker.

After the pasta, we cleared away the dishes and it was time for dessert. Well, at least nothing can go wrong with this, I thought as I took a tub of ice cream from the freezer then found chocolate sauce and maple syrup to pour over it.

I found bowls, put everything on a tray and took it all through and put it on the table.

'Help yourself,' I said to Luke. 'It's vanilla. Homemade by Mum.'

'Fantastic,' said Luke digging in with a large spoon. 'You can't beat that homemade flavour.'

'What do you think?' I asked as he took a mouthful.

'Erum . . .' I could see he was struggling to be polite, but it was clear that he didn't like it.

Then Tony took a spoonful. 'Ey*uuck*!' He spat it back into his bowl. '*Nesta!* This isn't ice cream.' He picked up the tub and looked at the label, then he burst out laughing. 'This is the creamed cod that Mum made last Friday night. No one was very hungry remember? She freezed the leftovers.'

By this time I was purple with shame. Luke was going to think I was Queen of Stupid. Reigning bimbo champion. 'Oh, so sorry, sorry,' I blustered. 'I'll get the right tub.'

'Don't worry,' said Tony getting up. 'I'll get it. You stay.'

'I'll give you a hand,' said Lucy getting up to go with him.

I gave Luke a weak smile and tried to gauge what was going on his head. Not sure, I thought. He does look amused. But is this a good thing? Or a bad thing?

And that's when I did my pièce de résistance for the night. I leaned over to relight one of the candles while at the same time giving Luke my best seductive look. I was so busy gazing at him that I didn't notice that as I lit the match and leaned over, the candle flared and next thing I knew, I'd singed the front of my hair.

'Aghh,' I cried as I frantically blew the candle out then poured a glass of apple juice over my forehead.

Lucy came back in with the ice cream. 'What's that strange smell, like something's burning?'

'And why is Nesta trying to drink her juice through

the top of her head?' asked Tony. 'Mm. Great party trick, Nesta. Sorry about my sister, Luke, she has these strange turns. It's probably time for her medication.'

'She just singed her hair,' said Luke as I lifted my head. Juice dripped down my forehead into my eyes causing my mascara to run. I couldn't bear it another moment. They were all looking at me as though I was a clown and they were waiting for the next trick.

'Excuse me a second,' I said, then ran to my bedroom and dived on to my bed. A second later, Lucy came after me.

'You OK?' she asked.

'Yes. Nooooo. I mean, can the evening get any worse?'

'No,' said Lucy sitting on the end of the bed and shaking her head solemnly. 'I don't think it can. But don't worry, everything happens in threes. You've had the three. The supper was raw. The ice cream was actually creamed *cod*. And you set fire to your hair. So that's one, two, three.' She tried to look concerned, but I could see it coming. Her shoulders were starting to shake. Then she bent over laughing. 'Snnnckkkk,' she giggled. 'Set . . . fire . . . to . . . your . . . hair.'

I began to see the funny side of it as well. 'Well Tony did tell Luke that my cooking would be an experience he'd never forget.'

'Oh you can be sure of that,' Lucy said, laughing. 'And I just knew there was something fishy about that ice cream.'

'Yeah, like, oh my cod,' I said and started laughing as well.

Soon the two of us had rolled off the bed and were on the floor howling, tears pouring down our cheeks. It wasn't long before Tony and Luke came to find out where we were.

At first Tony looked really concerned. Then he realised we were laughing, not crying.

'What's so funny?' asked Tony.

'Nesta is,' said Lucy pointing at me. 'Nesta Williams. The Domestic Coddess.'

And then they started laughing and Luke sat on the floor next to me and interlocked his hand with mine. It felt great. Like a current of electricity coursing right from the tip of my fingers to the tips of my toes.

After that the evening was brilliant. We went back into the sitting room, had ice cream with all the toppings we could find, maple syrup, chocolate sauce, chopped nuts and flakes and we played the chill out CD again. We were having such a good time that, before I knew it, it was ten-thirty and Mum and Dad were back.

Great, I thought. I'd been hoping that Luke would still be here when Dad got back. So maybe I didn't dazzle him with my brilliant cookery skills, but I was sure that Dad would impress him by chatting to him about films.

But something really weird happened instead.

Mum and Dad came in and Dad took one look at

Luke, then did a double take. Then he started staring at Luke with a really hard look on his face. What is the matter with him, I thought? It was like he had seen a ghost.

'Mum and Dad, this is Luke. Luke, this is Mum and Dad,' I said.

Mum smiled. 'Pleased to meet you, Luke. How was the curry?'

That set us all off laughing again.

'Hmm. Slight change of plan,' said Tony. 'Explain later.'

'Oh. OK,' said Mum, looking puzzled.

'And by mistake, I served your creamed cod as ice cream,' I said.

Mum started laughing then, but Dad was still staring at Luke.

'What's your surname, Luke?' he suddenly asked.

'De Biasi,' said Luke.

Dad's face clouded and he turned and left the room.

This wasn't like my dad. Usually he was King of Charm. Even Mum looked surprised by his behaviour. What was going on?

Nesta's Mum's Tips for Dinner Parties

- Keep it simple.
- If possible, have a trial run on a night before the dinner party, so that you know exactly what to do and how the meal will turn out.
- Choose a recipe where you can do most of the preparation beforehand and just heat it up when the guests arrive. That way, you can spend time with your guests.

Nesta's Tips for Dinner Parties

- Remember to turn on the oven.
- Read the labels on tubs in the freezer.
- Try not to burn your hair or eyebrows.

On second thoughts:

Nesta's Tips for Dinner Parties, Version Two

- Go out to eat.

Chapter 9

Old Misery

I confronted Dad in the kitchen the following morning.

'But why not?'

'Because I don't wish to, Nesta,' said Dad. 'And that's the end of it.'

'But Dad, you *have* to give me a reason . . .'

If Dad's face was a weather forecast, it just turned from clouds to thunder. 'I don't *have* to do anything,' he said.

I know teenagers are renowned for saying it's not fair, but this *really* wasn't. All I'd asked was that Dad be friendlier to Luke in future and chat to him about being a film director. But no, Old Misery was being, well, an old misery.

'But Dad, all I'm asking is that you talk to him. I felt ashamed of you last night, I really did. I've been brought up to be polite to visitors and make them feel welcome. Your behaviour was rude and for no reason.'

A loud snigger came from the counter where Mum was peeling carrots for Sunday lunch. She turned and looked at Dad with an amused look as if to say, 'Get out of that one, matie.'

Dad pouted like a sullen teenager. 'I don't wish to discuss it, Nesta. And for once in your life, will you please not question everything.'

'But it doesn't make sense. I don't understand. Give me a good reason. Luke's not a drug addict. Or a creep. Or an alien. So why? I don't understand why.'

'Subject closed,' said Dad, then he picked up his newspaper and held it up to his face.

Mum shrugged her shoulders and pulled an 'I don't know' kind of face. I went into the hall, grabbed my coat and headed for the front door.

'Where are you going?' called Mum. 'Lunch won't be long.'

'Lost my appetite,' I said as I opened the door then slammed it behind me.

As I made my way down the street, I felt tears sting the back of my eyes. I felt angry. And frustrated. And upset. I got on really well with my dad normally and we rarely argued. Why was he being so unreasonable all of a sudden? I didn't understand. I hate feeling like this, I thought, and I hate us not getting on at home. I called

Izzie on my mobile to commiserate. I knew she'd understand as sometimes she doesn't get on with her mum.

'Maybe it's a jealousy thing,' she said. 'Fathers never like to see their little girls with boys. He's always been your number one, then along comes a boy like Luke to steal you away. I mean, I know you've had cute boyfriends before, but Luke is exceptionally good-looking.'

'He is, isn't he?'

'Yeah. As in ding *double* dong. He looks a bit like Tony in fact.'

'Does not.'

'Does. In that he's very good-looking in an Italian kind of way. You know dark and . . .'

'Oh. Do you think I'm being all shallow and just going for looks again?'

'Dunno. Are you?'

'Well, I do like the way he looks, who wouldn't? But I can really talk to him as well. We get on. He knows a lot.'

'There you go then, Nesta. Beauty and brains. What more could you want?'

'Dad to like him.'

'Give him time. Maybe seeing Luke reminded your dad that he's getting older. Who knows what goes on in our parents' warped and twisted minds? Maybe he's going through the male menopause. How did Luke react when your dad gave him the cold shoulder?'

'Disappointed, I think. He'd been really looking

forward to talking to him about movies. I felt such an idiot. I'd given my dad this great build up then he turns up, and blanks Luke. He split soon after Dad got home. He knew that he wasn't welcome.'

'Weird, huh? Your dad's never been heavy about a boy before.'

'I know.'

'So what are you going to do?'

'I'm going to see Luke right now. He told me he was working at Biasi's today, so I'm just going to pop in and check that he's cool.'

'Er, Nesta. Are you sure you should?' asked Izzie. 'I mean, you're always the first to say don't be too available in the beginning of a relationship. You invited him for dinner last night and now you're going to see him again. Might be too much, too soon, don't you think? Might frighten him off.'

'Nah. This is different. I think he needs to know that I'm on his side, not on my dad's. Besides, I know he likes me. Even though he left pretty fast last night, we did have a snog at the door before he went.'

'Out of ten?'

'Ten. He's an ace kisser.'

'Not a brace kisser?' said Izzie with a laugh.

'Nope. I was worried about my brace at first, but it didn't get in the way at all, and he did say to go in and see him if I felt like it.'

'Well, good luck,' said Izzie. 'And I hope your dad chills. Try talking to him again when he's had a bit of space. He probably realises that he was out of order last night and will be more receptive to talking later.'

Good old Izzie, I thought. She's always good to chat to in a crisis. She's sort of calm and wise at the same time. And mad as well, if that's possible. 'Yeah, right, I will,' I said. 'I think that's why I was so upset, as we've always been able to talk about stuff before, but this time, it was like he put up a brick wall.'

The atmosphere in Biasi's was brilliant. The place was packed and buzzing with lunch-time diners and, although Luke was busy serving people, I could tell that he was pleased to see me.

'I'll catch you on my break in about fifteen minutes,' he said as he directed me to a bar counter near the till where a large, glamorous, dark-haired lady was sitting with a glass of red wine.

'Mum, this is Nesta,' he said.

His mum was great. Within minutes she was telling me all about her family, and the village in Italy she came from, and the house that they have there where they grow olives and herbs and make their own pesto. When I told her that I was half Italian, she treated me as if I were a long lost relative and insisted that I have the recipe for their pesto along with a sample jar. After ten minutes or so, we were joined by a very suave-looking older man with silver-grey hair.

'Dad,' mouthed Luke from the other side of the restaurant. He didn't need to tell me. I could see immediately as they were the spitting image of each other.

Like Mrs De Biasi, Luke's dad was very friendly and charming. He insisted that I have a drink on the house and sample the olives and freshly baked bread while I waited for Luke.

As I sat there munching, Marisa came out of the kitchen in the back carrying a birthday cake with loads of candles. Complete pandemonium broke out as Mr and Mrs De Biasi led the waiters with trumpets and tambourines in a chorus of 'Happy Birthday' sung to a white-haired old lady who was dining with her family. I felt so at home and it seemed that everyone who came into the restaurant felt the same way. Most of the diners knew the De Biasis personally and Mrs De Biasi relished filling me in on all sorts of gossip and who was who and who did what.

Luke came and sat with me in his break and his mum and dad made themselves scarce, but not before his mum gave me a huge wink.

'I really like your parents,' I said. 'Meeting them makes me feel extra bad about last night and my dad. He's not usually like that.'

Luke shrugged. 'Maybe he wasn't feeling well. Another time. In fact, bring your mum and dad down here for a meal. As you can see it's pretty informal and relaxed around here.'

'That's a great idea,' I said. 'Dad's bound to love it. I mean, he *is* Italian. He loves good pasta. He'll love the atmosphere in here and so will Mum.'

'Any time,' said Luke.

I glanced over at his dad. 'Your dad seems really nice and approachable. Why don't you try telling him about wanting to act.'

Luke put a finger up to his mouth as if to hush me. He indicated a few of the other waiters and waitresses busy rushing about dealing with the Sunday lunch crowd. 'I have tried, believe me. But see the staff. A few of them are actors. Like William over there, he hasn't worked since last year . . .'

'I thought I recognised him,' I said. 'He was in . . . oh, I can't remember the name of it, a soap on ITV?'

Luke nodded. 'Yeah. His face was everywhere, but since then nothing has come in.'

'Yeah, but he was, like, *really* famous. I'd have thought producers were queuing up for him.'

Luke shook his head. 'He says that so many of his actor friends are resting. Basically that means out of work.' He pointed at a girl with short red hair busy carrying plates of tiramisu. 'That's Sophie. Also an out of work actor. See, Dad gets to see so many of them here as they come and ask for work whilst they're in between jobs. He doesn't want that for me.'

'But hasn't that put you off?'

'Nope. I understand that you don't get every job and that there are periods when you don't work. I'm not under any illusion that you become an actor and, hey presto, everyone wants you. No. I will help out in Dad's restaurants, it's just . . . I don't want it to be my whole life. My only career. Acting will always be my number one, but I'm well aware that you have to have backup as well.'

What he said made me think. Dad was always saying the same thing – that work in the media often meant feast or famine, our family had enough experience of it ourselves, but I hadn't related it to myself before and thought about a backup career. I'd just presumed that it would be different for me, that I'd have loads of work when I hit the stage, but maybe it wasn't going to be as easy as that.

'So you see why Dad isn't that enamoured when I tell him that I want to be an actor when I leave school?'

I nodded. 'Yes, but I guess it's because he cares about you. Wants you to be secure and all that . . .'

'Yeah. But I want to be happy as well.'

'Dads, huh?'

Luke nodded. 'Yeah. A pain.'

'Yeah. But it's not usually a pain with my dad. He's great most days. In fact, I'm going to go home and have it out with him. And I think you should with your dad, too.'

'Yeah, right,' said Luke. 'How about you go with yours first and you can tell me how it went next Wednesday.'

Mum, Dad and Tony were just finishing lunch when I got home over an hour later laden with presents.

'What's all this?' asked Mum as I emptied my carrier bag out on the kitchen table.

'Cool,' said Tony as he picked up a packet of almond biscuits.

Mrs De Biasi had given me a huge Panettone, biscuits, jars of anchovies, a bottle of olive oil, a jar of pesto.

'From Luke's mum,' I said. 'She's amazing. When she found out that I was half Italian, she wouldn't stop giving me things. I tried to refuse, but she insisted, saying that it was all from the restaurant so not expensive. And Mr De Biasi said that I must bring you all there.'

Dad looked up from his plate.

'Look Dad, all your favourites . . .' I continued.

'So you met Mr De Biasi?' interrupted Dad.

'Yeah. He's really nice. You'd really like him. He's very handsome like you. Luke's mum's very good-looking as well. Glam in a Sophia Loren kind of way. So when shall we go?'

Dad got up from the table. 'I'd prefer it if you didn't see Luke or go there again,' he said, then he left the room.

I was gobsmacked. I looked at Mum and Tony. They

looked surprised as well, but neither of them said anything. The silence felt really uncomfortable.

'What *is* going on?' I asked. 'What's the matter with Dad?'

'Beats me,' said Tony.

Mum sighed and looked after Dad. 'I think . . . I think your dad should tell you.'

'Tell me what? You're not getting divorced are you?' I gasped.

'No, silly.'

'Is it because there isn't much money at the moment?'

Mum shook her head.

'So what then?'

Mum sighed. 'Look, I'll tell you part of the story, but then you must ask your dad.'

I sat down at the table. 'OK. Listening.'

'Your dad knew Luke's dad. Years ago. I never met him, it was long before we were together, but I've heard him talk about him. Gianni De Biasi. Apparently they were mates when they were lads, in fact, more than mates from what I can make out. They were like brothers.'

'Ohmigod! It's true what they say, it's a *small* world. Well that's *brilliant*, isn't it? They can meet up again. It will be soooo fantastic.'

Mum shook her head. 'No. Something happened . . .'

'What?'

'That's the part I think your dad should tell you,' she said.

Mrs De Biasi's Homemade Pesto
(serves four)

3 handfuls of fresh basil (finely chopped)
1 handful of pinenuts (lightly toasted)
1 handful of Parmesan cheese (grated)
Quarter of a clove of garlic
Lemon juice
Extra virgin olive oil
Sea salt and freshly ground black pepper

Pound the garlic, a pinch of salt and the basil in a bowl. Add the pinenuts and pound again. Add half the Parmesan. Stir, then add just enough olive oil to bind the sauce.

Season with salt and pepper to taste, then add the rest of the cheese. If you're not happy with the consistency, keep adding oil and cheese until you are. Add a squeeze of lemon at the end.

Delicious mixed into pasta.

Chapter 10

Oh, Brother!

'So what *did* happen with them?' asked Lucy.

We were sitting in the playground at break the next morning. TJ, Lucy, Izzie and me, squashed on a bench trying to keep warm as it was a cloudy day with a bitter wind blowing.

'Still don't know. I was about to go charging in to Dad and find out the rest of the story, but Mum asked me to let him tell me in his own time. Somehow I got the feeling she was right. It wasn't the time to start demanding answers. I've never seen Dad like this before and it wasn't so much that he was angry, more like upset.'

Lucy nodded. 'I think you were right. Mum says you can't force people to talk until they're ready. In fact, forcing an issue that is very painful may only make someone bury it deeper.'

'I guess I just have to wait then,' I said.

'Poo,' said Izzie.

'I know.'

'But we don't know it was painful,' said Izzie. 'All we know is that something happened.'

'Sounds a biggie whatever it was,' said TJ. 'A mystery. I wonder what it is.'

'So do I,' I said. 'The suspense is killing me and patience is not my best virtue.'

'Maybe they were both in love with Luke's mum,' said Lucy looking dreamy. 'You said she was glamorous. If she still is now, then she was probably even more stunning when she was younger. Maybe she was your dad's childhood sweetheart then Luke's dad stole her away and your dad has never forgiven him.'

'You've been watching too many romantic videos, Lucy,' I said.

'Or maybe it was *your* mum that they both wanted,' said TJ.

I shook my head. 'No. Mum said they knew each other before she came on the scene.'

'Maybe Tony's mum then,' said TJ, then gasped. 'Maybe he murdered her! That would give your dad good reason not to want to see Luke's dad.'

'She died in hospital, bozo,' I said. 'She was ill. And if

he'd murdered her, er, don't you think he might be in prison? Not running a chain of Italian restaurants.'

'Oh yeah, sorry, got carried away,' said TJ. 'Well, whatever the reason, I reckon it must have been about love. Most of these types of things are.'

'Or money,' said Izzie. 'Maybe they were in business together and one of them did the dirty.'

'I don't think so,' I said. 'My dad wouldn't and Luke's dad looks pretty decent.'

'It might have been something really small,' said Lucy. 'A misunderstanding that was never resolved.'

'It's just like *Romeo and Juliet*,' said TJ. 'Remember? The Montagues and Capulets, they were both Italian, just like you, both families hated each other and Romeo and Juliet were forbidden to see each other, just like you and Luke.'

'Thanks a lot, TJ,' I said. 'They both end up dead if I remember right.'

'Only because everything went wrong with their getaway plan,' she said. 'Juliet pretends to be dead and Romeo thinks that she actually is, so he kills himself, then she wakes up, sees that he's dead and kills herself as well.'

Lucy rolled her eyes. 'Not a comedy, then?' she asked.

'No,' I said. 'And I can't stand all that boring thee, thou and forthwith stuff.'

'*Nesta!*' said TJ. 'It's one of Shakespeare's most famous plays. It's a fab story. There's a movie with Leonardo Di

Caprio as Romeo that's worth watching if you don't want to read the play itself.'

Oh, here we go again, I thought. I'm being got at just because I don't read as much as the others. 'Shakespeare schmakespeare. Sorry, TJ, I just don't think me and old Willie speak the same language.'

'You don't know until you've tried,' said TJ.

'Poo,' I said.

'Maybe Luke will remember something,' said Lucy. 'Maybe he's heard your dad's name when his dad has been talking about the past.'

'But your dad doesn't want you to see Luke,' said TJ. 'Are you going to disobey him?'

'Well, I'm going to go to my acting class and oh, *quelle surprise*! Luke just happens to go as well. Tony knows I met Luke at acting class, but Mum and Dad don't. What they don't know, won't hurt them.'

'Text us as soon as you find out anything, oh Juliet,' said TJ as the bell for classes rang summoning us back to lessons.

It was great to see Luke again on Wednesday in the acting class and this time he was there right on time.

'I need to talk to you later,' I whispered to him as Jo asked us all to stand in the centre of the room for warm-up exercises.

After a few stretches and a bit of limbering up, we went

on to an improvisation where we had to get into groups of three, then act out a scene showing two people that got on well and didn't like the third person. First, Jo asked us to do the scene with dialogue and then again showing the same scenario with mainly body language. It was soooo interesting as, like the last class, it showed that the way people hold themselves can reveal more than what they say. It made me more determined than ever to walk upright and not slouched over like some saddo. I might not be able to smile with confidence any more, but I can at least walk as though I believe in myself.

Following that, we played games where we had to throw out suggestions for creatures and actions. Izzie said, 'Bees buzzing,' and we all had to pretend to be bees. Then, someone else said, 'Sheep grazing,' and we all had to do that. It was a real laugh, especially seeing all these middle-aged people acting like five-year-olds and rolling on the floor. It felt more like playschool than an acting class.

Then, Jo started putting newspaper on the floor.

'Twelve pieces,' she said, then counted the people in the class. 'Twelve of you. Go and stand on a piece of paper and I'm going to play some music. As the music plays, move around the floor only stepping on the paper. As you do so, I'm going to remove some of the paper, then I'm going to stop the music and I want you to freeze where you are. Anyone who has a foot on the floor is out.'

Definitely playschool, I thought as I found a piece of paper and the music started up. It was hysterical as, when the music stopped, we found that there were only eight pieces of paper left on the floor. Panic broke out as everyone scrabbled to stand on a piece of paper. A few people were out as they lost their balance and stood on the floor. And so it went on until there were four of us left and only two pieces of paper. Izzie, Luke, Jan and I. We had to really hang on to each other so that one of us didn't lose our balance and put a foot off the paper. For me, it was a great excuse to wrap myself around Luke. He didn't seem to mind at all and held on to me tightly. He smelled divine, sort of citrusy and warm and it felt great to snuggle into his neck with a legitimate excuse. Then Izzie started laughing as she had her leg wound around mine and was losing her balance and threatening to topple all of us over. That started me laughing as well and soon all four of us were giggling like idiots, desperately trying to hang on to each other at the same time and not lose our footing. As the music started up again and people began to unfold, I found that I couldn't. I seemed to be caught in Luke's jumper.

'Oh *no*!' I cried as Luke tried to move away. A strand of wool from his jumper had got caught in my brace, so I was attached to his neck like a Siamese twin. 'Enuheraahh . . .'on't 'ove.'

Jo saw what was happening and rushed over to separate

us, but I felt so embarrassed. All the rest of the group was standing laughing. Even Luke thought it was hilarious. 'My animal magnetism,' he said grinning, as Jo carefully extricated the wool I'd caught on from my brace. 'Girls just can't bear to be apart from me.'

I felt stupid. I had spent most of my time trying to talk through half closed lips so no one would notice my brace, then I went and did something that brought it to *everyone*'s attention. Like me saying, er, just in case you missed the fact that I have railway tracks on my teeth, watch this!

The rest of the class went without a hitch and it was fun, but I couldn't help checking my watch. I was looking forward to the end, so I could get Luke on his own.

At last it was over and, as we all trooped out of the school, Luke offered to give Izzie and me a lift home.

'Nice car,' said Izzie as he held the door open for us five minutes later. 'I like these Volkswagen Passats.'

I hadn't even noticed the car as I was so impatient to talk to Luke. Amazing that Izzie knew what type it was, I thought as I got into the front seat. When did she become a car expert? Up until recently, if you asked her about a car, she'd say, 'Oh, er . . . it was a green one.'

'So what was it you wanted to say to me?' asked Luke as he started up the engine.

'You won't believe it,' I said and quickly filled him in on my dad's weird reaction to hearing that I had met his dad and what my mum had told me about my dad and his being old friends.

'Wow,' he said. 'Small world, huh? And at least that explains why he did that double take on Saturday night. Like he'd seen a ghost.'

'I suppose he had in a way, if he used to be mates with your dad. You do look like him. But have you ever heard him talk about my dad? Matt Costello.'

'Don't think so.' Luke shook his head.

'Nan used to call Dad Matteo not Matt. Maybe your dad will know him as that.'

'I'll ask him when I get home. Try and find out what happened.'

After we'd dropped Izzie, Luke drove up to Highgate and we stopped in at Café Rouge for a late night hot chocolate. We soon got talking about films and, once again, I felt aware of how much he knew about them and I didn't. I decided to tell him about how I pretend I'm a character in a film if I'm in a stressful situation.

'So what character would you be now?' he asked.

'But I only do it when I'm stressed.'

'Yeah. So what character would you be now?'

'But what makes you think I'm stressed?' I asked.

'You're still holding your hand over your mouth. You *can* relax with me you know, the brace doesn't bother me.' Then he smiled. 'Except that is, when you fasten it to my left shoulder.'

I tried putting my hand down, but he was right, I couldn't relax. I couldn't help but be aware of my metal mouth.

'So what character?' he asked.

My mind had gone blank. 'Dunno,' I said.

'OK. Who are your top favourite characters in films then?'

I wanted to distract him. I felt really awkward. He was sitting so close and doing that lovely thing that some boys do – looking into your eyes and then at your mouth, then back at your eyes. Only I couldn't enjoy the sensation as I was so aware of how *un*attractive my mouth was. 'Don't you ever think about anything else besides movies?' I asked through closed lips.

He looked hurt for a moment. 'Yeah. Sorry. Was I being boring?'

'*No*. Just . . .'

'No, sorry . . . I know I can go on,' he said leaning back slightly and crossing his arms over his chest. 'I tend to get carried away. So. What would you like to talk about?'

I felt a sinking feeling in my stomach. I've blown it, I thought. I've cut him off when he was in full flow about his major passion in life. I've made him feel ill at ease. I can tell by his body language and the way he's crossed his arms, like closing off from me. I read somewhere that people do that when they feel uncomfortable. Maybe the girls were right when they said that I don't give boys a chance to show the true side of themselves. Right. That's it, I thought. I have to change and be able to hold a conversation about films without being intimidated by my lack of knowledge or else he's going to get bored with me. And I have to learn not to be inhibited about my teeth.

'No, sorry. I *am* interested in films just . . .' I glanced at my watch, 'Just . . . oh dentists. Look at the time, look I'd better . . .'

'Er, *dentists*?' Luke said, laughing. 'What have they got to do with anything?'

'It's my new swear word,' I said. 'Look. Sorry, but I'd better go. Mum thinks I've only gone to class so, if I'm any later, she'll worry.'

'And we don't want your dad to suspect you're out with me until we've got to the bottom of why my family is a no-go zone.'

'Exactly,' I said standing up, 'but he won't know that I'm out late. He's away at the moment, on location in Bristol. He's filming a two parter for the BBC there.'

'Cool.' Luke stood up and helped me put on my jacket. 'Let me pay for the drinks, then we'll go.'

While he was away at the counter, I took a look around the café and spotted Jade Wilcocks and Mary O'Connor from our class at a table on the far side. Jade caught my eye and waved me over.

'Hey, Nesta,' she said when I went to join them.

'Hey.'

'Is that the divine brother I keep hearing about?' asked Jade, jutting her chin in Luke's direction.

I shook my head. 'No. His name's Luke. Why would you think he's my brother?'

'Looks a bit like the guy I saw Lucy with in Hampstead once in the summer,' said Mary, 'and I knew she was seeing your brother off and on so . . .'

Then it hit me. That had to be it! The reason why Dad wanted me to stay away from Luke. Lucy had been right. It was a love thing. It was *obvious*. Izzie was right too, Luke did look a bit like Tony. Mary was right in mistaking them for each other. Which explained why Dad didn't want me to see Luke any more. Dad had clearly had a love affair with Luke's mum. Luke *was* my brother!

'Are you OK?' asked Mary. 'You look a bit faint all of a sudden.'

'Umf . . .' I said. Ohmigod. I'd snogged my own brother. And given him ten out of ten. Told Lucy that he was an ace kisser.

Now what, I asked myself as Luke came over to join us. My brain was about to explode.

'Luke,' I said. 'Sorry got to go.'

'Yeah. I'll give you a lift . . .'

'*No*. Can't see you any more. Sorry.'

Luke looked around the café. 'Did I just miss something? *Why* can't you see me any more?'

'Because you're my brother!' I blurted out.

'You just said he wasn't,' said Jade, who seemed to be enjoying every moment.

I headed for the door. 'Well he is,' I called over my shoulder. 'Sorry, Luke.'

And with that, I ran out of the café. As soon as I was outside, I dialled Dad's mobile.

> Top Tip for Brace Wearers
>
> When snuggling into a boy's neck or shoulder, if he's wearing anything made of wool, keep your mouth shut.

Chapter 11

Oops!

'Where's Mum?' I asked as soon as I got home.

'Having an early night. She's doing the morning shift tomorrow,' said Tony, who was slouched on one of the sofas in front of the telly in the sitting room. He was watching the sci-fi channel, currently his favourite.

I raced down the corridor into Mum's room, but the lights were out and I could see she was in bed.

'Mum,' I whispered in case she was still awake. No response, so I gently closed the door and went back to the living room.

'Tony . . .'

'Shhhhhhhh,' he said and turned up the volume on the remote.

'I need to . . .'

'*Nesta*. Don't be annoying.'

'It's *really* important . . .'

Tony's eyes didn't leave the screen. '*So* is this. Talk to me after. It's a *crucial* moment.'

'Can't you record it? I really need to talk to you.'

Tony turned up the volume even higher. '*Later.* Now *shut* up.'

He was starting to look cross, so I thought I'd better be quiet or else he'd get me back when I was watching *The Simpsons* or something that I like. Plus, I know how it feels when you're really stuck into a programme and someone comes in and starts talking away as though the telly's not even on. It's Dad usually.

I went to look on the kitchen notice board to see if Mum had put Dad's number up there. No. Nothing. Only taxis, pizza places and plumbers. This is really bad, I thought. No one seems to realise, this is an emergency and I can't get hold of my own father.

Finally, *finally,* Tony's programme ended and he turned to me and leaned forward. 'OK. You've got two minutes before the next episode starts. What's so important?'

'Luke. I think he's our brother. I need to talk to Dad.'

Tony fell back on the sofa laughing. 'Right. Yeah. Everyone's our brother, everyone's our sister. In fact, the world . . .' he began to sing, 'is just a great big family . . .'

'No, I'm serious Tone . . . Our half-brother. I think Dad had an affair with Luke's mum, then Mr De Biasi came along and pushed Dad out of the way and now they hate each other.'

'Are you on *drugs*?'

'No.'

When Tony saw that I wasn't laughing, he tried to make his face go straight. 'OK. Just what exactly makes you think this?'

'It's obvious, Tony. Think about it. Dad doesn't want me to see Luke. He blanches when I mention that I've met Luke's dad . . .'

'Exactly,' said Tony. 'I was there. He went weird when you mentioned Luke's dad. Not his mum. Don't you think if he'd had this great affair with Mrs De Biasi that there might be some kind of reaction when you mentioned her?'

That stopped me for a moment. 'Yeah. No. The fight was with Mr De Biasi as he was the one who took Mrs De Biasi away from Dad. Maybe. Anyway. I need to speak to Dad.'

'He's in Bristol somewhere.'

'I *know*, dingbat. But where's his number? He always leaves his contact number.'

'Mum will have it.'

'Mum's asleep,' I said.

'Good, as it's probably not a good idea to call Dad out of the blue and tell him that you know about his secret *lurve* child.'

'It's not funny, Tony.'

'It is.'

'Isn't.'

'*Is*. You're mad to think that about Luke. Lost the plot. Away with the fairies. Barking. Woof. Woof.'

'Don't be horrible. What am I going to do?'

'You'll just have to wait, Nesta.' He flicked the volume back up for the next episode of his programme and stretched out again. 'Call him in the morning. In the meantime, get us a Coke will you?'

I threw a cushion at him, then got up to go to the kitchen. Sometimes I think Tony thinks I'm nothing more than his private slave. Two brothers? I don't know if I could cope.

I didn't sleep well that night. I dreamed that Dad was having supper with Marlon Brando. Both of them had braces on their teeth and kept singing that song that goes something like, 'We are familee, look at all my brothers and me . . .' All sung in a thick Italian accent.

As I staggered into the bathroom the next morning, I contemplated as to whether to ask Mum about Luke. It might come as a blow to her. She might not know anything about Dad having a secret child. I'd ask Dad to do the right thing and tell her himself. Yes, I thought. That would be best.

Mum and Tony were both already in the kitchen

having coffee and chatting when I went to grab some breakfast. I gave Tony a filthy look and turned to Mum. 'I need to talk to Dad. Can I have his number in Bristol?'

'Sure,' she said. 'It's on the pad next to the bed in my room. Give him my love, won't you.'

When I found the number, I sat on Mum's bed and dialled.

A female voice answered. 'Hello, Hogarth Hotel.'

'Can I speak to Mr Costello, please?'

The phone went quiet for a moment, then I heard a ringing, then the receptionist came back on again. 'I'm afraid there's no reply,' she said. 'Would you like to leave a message?'

'No thanks,' I said, then put the phone down. My heart was thumping and I realised that I hadn't really thought about what I was going to say and needed to plan how to put it. Like, hey, Dad about your secret son? I don't think so.

I was about to try his mobile when Mum came into the room and sat on the bed beside me. She was trying not to, but I could tell she was having a hard time not laughing.

'Nesta,' she said. 'Tony's just been telling me what you think about this boy Luke that you've met. Um, listen love, I can't let you go into school with this on your mind. He's not your brother, I can tell you that much. As I said on Sunday, your dad does have some history with Luke's dad and . . . he should have told you what it was all about himself.'

'Well, you tell me . . .'

Mum hesitated for a moment, then shook her head. 'Let your dad tell you when he gets back at the weekend. I'll have a word with him. I promise he'll tell you the whole story and, in the meantime, I can assure you that what he'll have to say is *not* that Luke is your brother or his son.'

'Promise?'

'Promise.'

'Because I *have* kissed him you know.'

I could see that Mum was struggling not to laugh and I could hear Tony sniggering in the corridor behind the door.

'Did you tell Dad he's been a very naughty boy and we know all about his love child?' he called through.

'You shut up, Tony pig face,' I called back.

He opened the door and leaned in. 'You've been watching too many soaps, Nesta. Now the *real* truth is that Mrs De Biasi is actually a transexual, but when she was a man, she fathered Lucy behind Mr Lovering's back. TJ is an alien and Izzie, well, we all know that she's had three babies and is trying to hide them from her mother. And Izzie's mum, well, she's actually a lesbian who's afraid to admit it and Mr Foster is on drugs but trying to reform.'

I went to throw one of the pillows from Mum's bed at Tony, but Mum stopped my arm. 'Now *stop* it, both of you. Enough of this nonsense. Nesta, you've got an over-vivid imagination. Tony stop winding her up. And *both* of you, off to school NOW.'

I got up and pushed past Tony, but not without sticking my tongue out at him and standing on his right foot with all my weight.

'Owwwww,' he cried. 'Muuuuum.'

'Baby,' I said.

'*Enough*,' said Mum getting up from the bed.

I went into the kitchen and grabbed a piece of toast off a plate on the breakfast bar, put on my jacket and headed off for school. Sometimes I hate having a brother. I'm glad I haven't got two, I thought. Ohmigod. What must Luke have thought? Oh dentists. I checked my mobile in the hope that there was a message from him. Nothing. Oh double dentists. I'd better phone and grovel. Apologise. Explain that . . . what will I say? That aliens came to Highgate last night and took over my brain for a couple of hours? Oh dear. I suppose it was a bit mad thinking that he was my brother, but it made sense at the time. Triple dentists. I must work on my excuses and come up with a really good one if I'm to get him back. Oh, knickers. Sometimes it's very difficult being me.

Nesta's Excuses for Having Acted Crazy

1) Aliens landed and took over my brain for two hours.
2) No! That wasn't me. That was my psychotic twin. We don't usually let her out, but she escaped last night for a short while. Soooooo sorreeeeeeeeeeeeee.
3) Pretend to be an actress and say: 'I was researching a role for my new movie where I have to play a mad girl and I wanted to get into the character for a while.'

Chapter 12

Mental Makeover

I dialled Luke's mobile on the way to school. It was switched off.

I tried again when I got to school. Still switched off.

In the break at school, I made my way into the girls' cloakroom, found a cubicle then dialled his number again. Luckily it was break at his school as well, as he picked up.

'Hi, this is Nesta,' I said.

'Oh. Yeah. Hi.' His voice sounded cold. Uninterested.

'I er, just wanted to say three things. First sorry, the aliens got me. Not my fault I was weird last night, they interfered with my brain.'

There was silence at the other end.

'OK. Not aliens. Um . . . I was researching for a film role where I have to play a schizophrenic. That's someone with a dual personality. No, you weren't. Yes, I was. Shut up. No, you shut up.'

Still silence.

'OK, you got me,' I said. 'I have to tell you the real truth. I have an evil and psychotic twin. It was her you saw last night.'

Still silence.

'Oh Luke, listen, I guess, I . . . I wanted to say, sorry. I guess I acted a bit strange last night. This thing with our dads has got to me more than I thought and my mum always said I had an overactive imagination. I guess it ran away with me. I know what I thought was mad especially now in the light of the day, having slept on it and . . .' I realised that I was doing all the talking. 'Are you still there, Luke? Join in anytime . . .' There was a very looooooooong silence. Oh dentists, I thought, I'm going to be dumped before we really got started. And it's all my stupid fault. 'Are you still there, Luke?'

'Yeah.'

'Right. So . . .' But I didn't have anything else to say. My flow of bad apology and mad excuses had dried up. 'Um, OK then. See you around maybe . . . Sorry, sorry . . .'

'Look, Nesta,' said Luke, 'I think you have to make up your mind what you want. I felt a total idiot last night, being left in that café with two of your mates watching it all . . .'

'Not my mates. They're in my class . . .'

'Whatever.'

'Yeah. Sorry. Whatever.'

'And what were you on about? Me being your brother?'

'I know. Oops. Big mistake. Velly solly.'

I heard the bell go in the distance at his end. 'I have to go to class. Look, Nesta. I think we got involved a bit fast. Let's slow down a bit and take some time. Think about what we want, OK. *You* think about what *you* want. I get the feeling that you don't really know.'

'Oh . . . OK.'

'Just take some time . . .'

'Yeah,' I said. 'I heard you. Take some time. OK. One, two, three. OK. Ready.'

At last Luke laughed. 'Bit longer maybe. Look. Call me later,' he said. 'Maybe we could meet up tomorrow?' This time his voice sounded warmer.

'OK. Later.'

Hurrah, I thought as I switched my phone off and went to find the girls. Once again, life never closes a wotsit without opening another wotsit.

Tomorrow, he'd said. That's Friday. In that case, I decided, I was going to take full advantage of the next twenty-four hours and put myself through a mental makeover and crash course on films and all I could find to do with them. When I saw Luke next, I was going to astound him with my tip-top knowledge of everything to do with movies and not just the entertaining kind that I liked. I was going to be Miss Film Critic of the year.

At lunch-time, I went to the library and piled all the books about films that I could on to the desk. I poured through them trying to remember who'd directed what and who'd produced what, so that I could name-drop and impress Luke. In the evening, I pulled all Dad's movie books out on to the dining table and continued my swotting up.

'What's going on?' asked Tony when he found me nose to page with *Halliwell's Film Guide*.

'Need to know about movies,' I said, indicating the books.

'But you do already,' he said. 'Don't tell me that having a director as a dad hasn't rubbed off on you? I think you know more than you realise.'

'Not as much as Luke. He knows about ones I've never heard of.'

'And you probably know about ones he's never heard of. Don't put yourself down, Nesta.'

'But there's so many, hundreds, thousands, I'm beginning to think that there aren't enough hours in the week to mug up on it all. I don't know where to begin.'

'Well what genre are you looking at?' he asked. 'You do know what a genre is, don't you?'

'Yeah. Course,' I said. 'It means type. Like romance or comedy. There are loads of different genres. Like thriller, horror, detective, sci-fi, war, cartoon . . .'

'See. You're not as stupid as you look,' said Tony.

'But I'll *never* have enough time to swot up on all of them,' I said, groaning. 'It's so complicated.'

'So why are you looking at all this stuff? For a school project?'

'No way. For Luke.'

Tony laughed. 'Ah well, there's only one film you should talk to him about,' he said.

'Which is?'

'The Coen brothers movie. *O Brother, Where Art Thou?*'

'Oh ha ha, you're so funny,' I said. 'I'm trying to forget about that minor brain blip. But seriously, I need to impress Luke with my knowledge of movies.'

'Why?'

'It's his passion and I think I blew it the other night by dismissing him when he was talking about them.'

'Ah. You've forgotten the rules.'

'What rules?'

'How to be a brilliant conversationalist.'

'I know how to be a brilliant conversationalist, least no one's ever complained before. Why? Do you know something I don't?'

'Actually, yes I do,' said Tony. 'Or something you've forgotten.'

'OK, Mister Know It All. What?'

Tony shook his head and looked at me sadly. 'Wow. This guy has really got to you, hasn't he? I don't think I've ever seen you lose it like this before. It's like your brain has gone dead. You don't talk, you *listen*. Ask a few pointed questions, then listen some more.'

'Duh? Explain?'

'What's the most flattering thing in the world?' asked Tony.

'To be told you're totally beautiful, I guess.'

'Wrong. Well, that's OK, but actually, it's when someone is like, totally interested in what you have to say. Often in conversations, people don't listen to each other. Not really. Often, all the time one person is talking, the other person is planning what they're going to say, often not even really listening . . .'

I couldn't resist. 'Sorry. What were you saying? I was too busy planning what I was going to say next.'

'If you're not going to pay attention . . .'

'No, Tone, I was just having a laugh. Sorry. Listening.'

'Well, that's it really. There's nothing more flattering than someone really listening to you. People *love* to talk about themselves and what they think. Course, this tactic won't last for ever, as you might get bored out of your brains listening to someone else's opinion all the time, but in the beginning it can really sway things in your favour. I do it all the time. Makes girls feel really special. A lot of boys haven't cottoned on to it yet. Ask girls what they think about things they're into and really listen like you're fascinated.'

I pointed to all the books I'd been studying. 'So you're saying that I don't have to study all this stuff?'

'You can if you want to but, if the only reason you're doing it is to have a conversation with Luke about movies and make him feel good, then you don't need to read up. All you need to do is listen to what he thinks, ask him his opinion about a few films and really listen to his replies. If you do it right, he won't even notice that you haven't said much.'

'Thanks Tony, you're a star,' I said. How could I have forgotten the golden rules, I asked myself? I already *knew* what he'd told me. Clearly falling in lurve had not made me blind but *stupid*. But then, I guess this is the first time that the tables have turned on me. Usually it's boys who are trying to impress me. I've never felt that I had to work hard to impress one of them before. And now Tony's reminded me how easy it is. Just let them talk and I listen. I put away the books and settled down to watch *EastEnders*. Bliss.

The Bluffer's Guide to Good Conversation, by Tony

1) When you can, bluff it.
2) When you can't, don't be afraid to say that you don't know about a subject or else you can end up looking a prat.
3) Third option is to feed lines to the person you're interested in and listen to their replies. Remember it only works in the short term. If you're really interested in someone for the long run, it's best to be honest, as communication has to be two-way for it to work.
4) Before you try option 3, practise until perfect, the kind of facial expression that says that you know exactly what he/she's talking about (a cross between glee and constipation).
5) Study your subject and start off with a few general openers that will spark off areas of interest eg, for film: 'And who do you think should win Best Actor at this years Oscars?'
6) Learn to feed lines that get him/her going on his favourite subject.

For example, for a boy who's into movies:

Right approach:

He: Are you into movies?

You: Oh yes. What are your top three favourites and why?
Him: Ten minutes animated reply.
You: Mmmm. *Fascinating.* Tell me more.
Him: Another ten minute animated opinion.
You: *Exactly!*
He: (thinks) What an impressive girl!

Wrong approach:
He: Are you into movies?
You: I prefer telly. Let me tell you what I think . . . (ten minutes of you talking.)
He: But I don't watch those things . . .
You: Really? Well let me fill you in on what you've been missing. (Ten minutes about the soap.)
He: (thinks) We have nothing in common, plus I can't get a word in. I'm outta here now.

Note from Nesta: Of course, true communication is two-way with talking and listening on both sides, but this is an excellent method when you are trying to pull, especially if you have a brace in, as it means you can just nod and look interested (and beautiful).

Chapter 13

Revelations

By Friday night, I was ready to try out my tip-top conversation skills on the lovely Luca. He called me on my mobile at lunch-time and asked if I'd like to go over to his house that evening.

'Mum will be here for a while,' he said, 'then she'll go to join Dad at the restaurant and Marisa's out with her mates, so I thought we could watch a movie or something.'

I'd like to do 'or something', I thought and almost said so, but I managed to restrain myself and put my 'How to be a brilliant conversationalist' into practice instead.

'I have to work for an hour or so at Lucy's dad's shop after school, but I could come over after that. A movie sounds great. But what genre? Sci-fi, Horror? War? Which do *you* prefer?'

Woah! Did that get Luke going! He was off and didn't pause for breath for five minutes.

'Mmmm. Exactly,' I said when he'd finished.

'I'm really looking forward to seeing you again,' he said. 'It's not often I meet a girl who knows about films and who I can talk to like this.'

Bingo, I thought. Hoho haha, yep yeppity yes.

After my shelf stacking stint at Mr Lovering's shop, I dashed home to get changed to go to Luke's. Black jeans, black polo neck, black kohl on my eyes, so that I looked like one of those Frenchie bohemian intellectual types. I made sure that I wore my high black boots though, so I didn't look too brainboxy.

I was ready to leave at the same time as Mum, who was going to pick up Dad from the station, and she offered to drop me on her way. She wasn't too happy when I gave her Luke's address.

'What's all this about then?' she asked as we followed the directions he'd given. 'I thought your dad asked you not to see him.'

'I know, but you haven't forbidden me, have you? And anyway, it doesn't make sense. Surely you can see that?'

'I guess.' Mum shrugged as if to say she didn't understand Dad's ultimatum either.

'Don't tell him where I am, will you?' I asked as we reached Luke's road and Mum stopped in front of a semi-detached house with a neat lawn in the front.

'Not if you don't want,' she said, 'but I think you two have got some talking to do over the weekend. I don't like all this going behind each other's backs and not telling the whole story . . .'

'He started it.'

Mum sighed. 'He has his reasons.'

'So why doesn't he tell me them?'

Mum sighed again. 'Just be back around ten, OK?'

'OK. Luke will probably drop me.'

'Well, give me a ring if he can't.'

Two minutes later, a smiling Mrs De Biasi opened the door of their house, then showed me into the sitting room. It was a Mediterranean-style room, modern with marble floors and light sofas dotted with turquoise and sea blue cushions. I did 'Polite Visitor' for a while and asked questions about the décor, how her week had been and so on, then she went to call Luke and get us some juice. As soon as Luke came down, I quickly asked if he had any update on the story of our two dads.

He shook his head. 'Not really, the time hasn't been right. There's either been people around or, I dunno . . . we don't exactly communciate very well at the best of times and I thought it might be weird if I suddenly asked about his past, especially if it's something awkward. How about you?'

I shook my head. 'Dad's only getting back this evening and I didn't think it was a question for the phone. But

Mum said she'd make him tell me the whole story. I'll let him have a lie-in tomorrow then see how it feels . . .'

Luke nodded. 'I know. Waiting for the right time can take forever sometimes . . .'

Suddenly I spotted a group of framed photos on the bookshelves at the back of the room and got up from the sofa to go and have a closer look. One of them was of a boy, who looked about ten. 'Ah sweet,' I said to Luke. 'It's you, isn't it?'

'It is,' said Mrs De Biasi coming back in with a tray of drinks and almond biscuits. 'He was such a sweetie.' She showed me another photo of a baby. 'And this is him as a baby.'

Luke looked really embarrassed. 'Muu*um*,' he groaned. 'What time are you going? I'm sure Nesta isn't in the least bit interested in looking at photos of me.'

I laughed. 'Oh, but I am. I love looking at photos and you were sooooo cute.'

'My lovely Luca,' said Mrs De Biasi, giving Luke's cheek a pinch. 'He was so beautiful as a child. A little cherub.'

'Mu*uum*,' groaned Luke again.

'You like to see some more, Nesta?' asked Mrs De Biasi pulling out some huge photo albums out from the shelf.

Luke went over to his mum and put a cautionary hand on her arm. '*No*, Mum. *Please*.'

'But I'd love to see them,' I said. 'Honest.'

Luke sighed and stepped out of the way. 'She does this all the time. Ma, I'm sure Nesta isn't in the slightest bit interested.'

Mrs De Biasi ignored him and laid two albums out on the coffee table. Soon we were sitting side by side and she was flicking the pages, showing me photos of Luke at six months, as a toddler, a little boy . . .

'Mum has photographed every event for every year since . . . the beginning of time,' said Luke indicating the shelves. 'See – all that bookcase is full of her albums, photos of relatives, friends, the milkman, the newspaper boy, everyone goes in.'

'People are what make life special,' smiled Mrs De Biasi. 'And now I am going to photograph you. It's not often Luke invites a girl home. Hold on, I'll just get my camera, I think it's upstairs . . .'

'Have you told your mum anything about my dad recognising your name?' I asked when she'd gone.

Luke shook his head. 'Didn't want to until we knew what it was about ourselves.'

'Probably best,' I said and went to look at the other framed photos on the bookshelf. 'Hey, are all these albums your mum's? Or is there one of your dad's?'

'Most of them are mixed,' said Luke getting up. 'But I seem to remember that there is one of Dad's from when he was young. Oh right. You think there might be a photo of your dad in there?'

I nodded.

'Smart thinking,' said Luke. 'Here. Let me find it.'

He found a tattered red album on the bottom shelf and hauled it on to the table. As he turned the pages, old sepia photos were revealed.

'Old aunties and great grandparents . . .' he said as faces from another era gazed out at us. About a quarter of the way through the book, the sepia pictures turned to black and white, then colour, then there it was.

'Ohmigod!' I gasped and pointed to a man in a photo. 'That's my dad.'

'And that's mine standing next to him,' said Luke.

The picture was of a couple of teenage lads sitting on a wall outside a terraced house. They looked about seventeen. Both had their arms round a teenage girl in the middle.

'Shhhh,' I said as we heard footsteps coming back down the stairs. 'Don't say anything. Let's see if she can tell us anything.'

'Hey Ma, who's this?' asked Luke, pointing at the photo. 'Not you, is it?'

Luke's mum came and stood next to him and looked at the picture. 'No,' she said, then smiled sadly. 'That was Matteo's sister, Nadia Costello.'

I looked closely at the photo. I'd seen pictures of Nadia, but not this one. I was almost named after her. She died when she was eighteen in a car accident, which is why Dad didn't want me to have the same name. Nesta was a sort of compromise to keep his mum happy.

'And who was Matteo?' asked Luke acting innocent.

Mrs De Biasi sat down at the table. 'He was your father's best friend. They grew up together. Like brothers they were.'

'Did you know him?' I asked.

'Oh yes,' she said. 'In those days, all the Italian families knew each other. We all lived close. We were in and out of each other's houses. We worked and played together. It was a very close community.'

'So how come I've never met him?' asked Luke playing it perfectly.

'Ah . . .' sighed Mrs De Biasi. 'They fell out.'

'Why?' asked Luke. 'What happened?'

'Nadia died,' said Mrs De Biasi, closing the album and putting it back on the shelf.

'But why would Matteo and Gianni fall out over that?' Luke asked.

'Matteo blamed Gianni for her death.'

'But why?' I gasped. 'What did he do?'

Mrs De Biasi sat on the sofa and looked out of the window for a moment, then she turned back to us. 'He didn't do anything. That's what is so sad. When Gianni was young, all the young Italians hung out together, all local . . .'

'Including Matteo's sister, Nadia?' I asked.

Mrs De Biasi nodded her head. 'One night, we'd all been to a club in Soho, Matteo was supposed to see Nadia home safely, but he'd just met some new girl. I can't remember her name. Oh, he was a one for the girls was Matteo . . .'

Like Tony, I thought. Like father, like son.

'He didn't want to be landed with his younger sister for the night,' continued Mrs De Biasi. 'He wanted to go off with his new girl. Anyway, he and Gianni argued about taking Nadia home and, as Gianni didn't have a girl that night, it was just before we dated, he agreed that he'd see her home. She had just passed her driving test and insisted on driving. I think Gianni had a bit of a crush on her and so he let her. Plus, she was a strong-willed girl was Nadia, I remember, liked to get her own way . . .' She was quiet for a few minutes and looked sad as though remembering something painful.

'So what happened?' I asked.

Mrs De Biasi let out a deep sigh. 'On their way home, some lunatic drunk driver ploughed into them. Nadia was killed instantly. and Gianni taken to hospital. We didn't know if he was going to make it as it was touch and go for him for a while. But Matteo never came to see him. He blamed Gianni and never spoke to him again.'

'But it wasn't Gianni, I mean Mr De Biasi's fault,' I exclaimed.

'No, it wasn't,' said Mrs De Biasi. 'But Matteo blamed him all the same.'

'Guilt,' I said. 'He was supposed to see her home, but went off with the other girl.'

'Yes.'

'What happened to him?' I asked. 'Do you know?'

'We heard that he married later,' said Mrs De Biasi, her eyes filling with tears. 'Had a son, then his wife died. So sad, so much loss in his life.'

Seeing Mrs De Biasi on the verge of tears caused tears to spring to my eyes. Poor Dad. Even though I knew about Nadia and of course about Tony's mum, I'd never really thought about how it must have been for him before. And now I felt really sorry for him. It must have been awful losing two people he was close to in such a short time.

'What was he like when he was young?' I asked.

Mrs De Biasi's face lit up. 'Oh he was a joy. So full of life. So charming. All the girls had a crush on him.' Her face clouded again. 'He moved away, to Bristol I think. That's the last we heard.'

I looked at Luke. I was dying to tell her that Dad only lived around the corner.

'Has Dad ever tried to contact him?' he asked.

'At first,' said Mrs De Biasi, 'but Matteo wouldn't have anything to do with him. I often wonder what happened to him. Gianni would dearly love to re-establish contact and heal the past.'

She pulled a tissue from her sleeve and had a good

blow. Then she sat up straight as though pulling herself together. 'Best not to dwell on the past. And anyway, why are you two so interested?'

I couldn't hold back any longer. 'Mrs De Biasi,' I burst out. 'I have something to tell you.'

Nesta's Top Tips for the Intellectual (But Sexy) Look

Clothes:

All black, tight fitting. Think Audrey Hepburn in the 1957 film classic, *Funny Face*. (Get my movie knowledge! Impressive or wot?)

No girlie pinks or pastels.

Accessories:

Pair of specs: even if you don't need them (preferably tortoiseshell and v. trendy frame).

Heavy-looking Russian novel (don't worry, you don't have to read it!).

Shoes: black chunky workman-type boots, but only if worn with ultra short skirt and black tights.

Packet of Gauloise cigarettes, but don't even think about lighting one up as they taste *dégoûtante* (disgusting).

Chapter 14

Surprise, Surprise!

I couldn't wait to tell Dad. Mrs De Biasi's reaction to discovering who I was had strengthened my resolve to get him and Mr De Biasi back together as soon as possible.

When she had grasped the fact that I really was Matteo's daughter, she laughed and hugged me, then cried, then rang her husband and cried and laughed all over again.

'Very emotional, my ma,' said Luke as we listened to her telling her husband the whole story over the phone. 'She cries at everything.'

'I think it's lovely,' I said. 'People shouldn't be afraid to show what they feel.'

'Gianni can't believe it,' said Mrs De Biasi after she'd put down the phone. 'We're both so pleased to know Matteo is well and happily married after so much tragedy early in his life. And so happy to know he has you and your brother Tony, but I fear that he won't have changed his mind about Gianni. I hope so, now that we have met you, Nesta, but don't get your hopes up, we have to respect his feelings too. We may want reconciliation but he may not.'

Luke nodded. 'Yes, it's really up to your dad,' he said.

'Well, what are your feelings, Mrs De Biasi?' I asked.

'Ah, Nesta. I feel that life is too short to hold these stupid grudges and those boys had a true friendship. Too precious to lose.'

Exactly my feelings, I thought. I couldn't imagine life without Lucy, Izzie and TJ to share everything with and talk things over with.

When Mrs De Biasi had gone off to the restaurant, Luke and I sat down to watch a movie. He'd already told me that he liked war films and, although they're not my favourite, I decided that, as part of my movie education, I had to expand my viewing and watch a few new genres. He'd picked out one called *Saving Private Ryan*. Should be OK, I thought, Tom Hanks is in it so it must be a feel-goody of a sort.

'It's really cool that you want to watch this,' said Luke as he put the DVD in the machine. 'Not many girls would, but I think it's important to know that these things went on.'

'Oh so do I,' I said as I took my boots off, then curled up on the sofa. I was feeling very pleased about everything. Happy happy. It was all going to turn out brilliantly. Even though Mrs De Biasi and Luke had their reservations, I was certain I was going to prove them wrong. I was going to reconcile Dad and Luke's dad. I could see the grand reunion now. It would be like those smaltzy programmes on telly that bring together people who have lost each other and they hug and cry, like Mrs De Biasi had, then clap and laugh and generally feel good and smile a lot. And it would all be down to me. Fab. And now, here I was with Luke ready to watch a serious-type film. Yes. I was definitely changing. Growing up. No one could accuse me of being shallow any more. Oh no, I reunite people, help heal troubled pasts and watch war films. You can't get more unshallow than that. Yeah. As the credits to the movie rolled, I wondered if I should get a pair of glasses to wear to complement my new persona. One of those pairs with square frames that make you look really cool and intelligent. I don't need glasses, but I'm sure I could get a pair without a prescription, just for the effect.

Luke and I snuggled up on the sofa and began to watch the movie. First five minutes, yeah, it was OK. Ten minutes, not really my cup of tea, but I'll sit through it for Luke. However, as it went on, I found I couldn't even do that. It was *horrible*. The war scenes were unbelievable, or rather they were totally believable. Awful. Graphic. People getting blown up and killed left, right and centre. I tried to make myself carry on watching, but it was too upsetting, so I made an excuse that I needed to use the bathroom and got out double quick.

As I splashed my face with water, I tried to tell myself that, as Luke had said, I ought to watch to know what went on. History and all that. Part of my education, etc. Then I thought, but I *do* know what went on. I do. Maybe I don't know names and dates and countries, but I do know what goes on in war. Hell on earth, that's what and it makes me *really* depressed. More than anything. Whatever nationality, I know mothers lost sons, sisters lost brothers, children lost fathers. Boys like Tony, Luke, Steve and Lal, hardly older and all sent to early graves. And I thought, why do people have to fight and kill like that? What for? Where's it got anyone? I truly believe that the majority of the world, of all races and beliefs, want to live in peace. They want to watch their pot plants grow on their patios, enjoy the summers, their families, their pets. I hate war. And I've just realised that I hate war films too.

After a few minutes, Luke came and knocked on the bathroom door.

'You all right in there?' he called.

I opened the door. 'Yes. No. Just . . . I'm really sorry Luke, but I can't watch any more of that film. I hope you don't think I'm shallow, but . . . I think there's so much bad news in the world, when I watch a movie I want to be entertained not freaked out . . .'

'Found it upsetting, did you?'

I nodded. 'Yeah. Sorry. Can't do it.'

Luke smiled. 'That's OK and I don't think you're shallow. Everyone likes different stuff, that's all. Look, I'll find you a feel-good movie instead. Ever seen *It's a Wonderful Life*?'

At last some of my swotting up came in handy. Only last night, I read about it in one of Dad's books. One of the great classics, the book had said. 'I haven't seen it, but it was directed by Frank Capra wasn't it? Starring James Stewart?'

Luke looked well impressed. 'Yeah. Hey, you know your stuff. Come on, I'll put it on for you.'

Ten minutes later we were back on the sofa and this time I got well stuck in. It was a fantastic movie. All about a man who feels his whole life has been a waste, until an angel takes him back through it, showing the effect he'd had on people and what would have happened if he hadn't been there. It was a really uplifting, amazing film and left me with a warm glow. Much better than seeing people get their heads blown off, I thought.

In their different ways though, both films made me think the same thing – that life is precious and it's really important to let the people that you love know it. Friends, family, whoever. Not to let any petty arguments or misunderstandings get in the way. By the end of the evening, I was certain that it was fated that I'd met Luke. It was my destiny to bring our dads back together. I couldn't wait.

Mum was sitting on her own in the sitting room when I got home. 'Where's Dad?' I asked.

'Oh, hi love. Bit of a crisis with the film. He had to go straight into the editing suite to sort it out. He'll be back later. There was some problem on the first rushes.' My face must have fallen as Mum looked at me anxiously. 'What is it, Nesta? What's happened?'

I went and sat beside her and the whole story poured out. 'You knew about Aunt Nadia, didn't you?' I asked.

'Some of it,' she admitted. 'Your dad told me about it once when we passed the place in North Finchley where they all used to live. I could tell it was a very sore subject for him. Look, I can see that you're dying to talk to him about it all . . . but not tonight sweetheart, please, he's got a lot on his mind with the film and probably won't be back until late. Let him sleep and you can talk in the morning.'

I did as I was told, but made sure I was up bright and early ready to break the news to him. Mum was right. I couldn't wait. I knew he'd be overjoyed that Mr and Mrs De Biasi wanted to see him and heal the past.

When I got to the kitchen, Mum was already making coffee.

'Can I take Dad's in to him?' I asked.

'Oh Nesta! You've missed him again. They didn't sort the problem last night, so he had to go in first thing. He was up at six. He said to say hi and he's sorry he missed you last night and he'll see you later. He'll probably be back before lunch.'

'Did you tell him that I know about the De Biasis?'

Mum shook her head. 'No, I didn't. Talk to him later . . . but Nesta, don't get your hopes up. I know you're excited about it, but your dad might not have the same reaction.'

'I bet he will,' I said. 'It's going to be fab. It all happened a long time ago. He's bound to want to see them again.'

Mum gave me a strange look, then went back to making toast.

Over breakfast, I told Tony the latest news and together we went to meet the girls and Luke in Costa in Highgate for mid-morning coffee and a general Saturday hang-out. We got there first, so bought some cappuccinos and pastries and looked for somewhere to sit.

'It's all starting to make sense now,' said Tony as he bagged our favourite seats in the window.

'What is?' I asked.

'Why Dad didn't want me to have driving lessons. Remember, he went over the top about it?'

I nodded. 'Yes, of course. Nadia had only just passed

her test when she was killed. I guess he didn't want anything like that to happen to you.'

Tony gazed out of the window for a while in silence. 'If he'd only told us what had happened, I would have understood. I really would. Instead, I thought he was being totally unreasonable . . .'

'I know,' I said. 'It's mad that we don't communicate properly. I mean, he's our dad. He ought to be able to tell us what he's really thinking. Oh, I do hope he'll see the De Biasis. I mean I understand he was freaked at the time, it was his responsibility to see Aunt Nadia home and he blew it, but he shouldn't blame it on Luke's dad.'

'No,' said Tony. 'But I guess you never think anything is going to happen like that. It's like, Mum and Dad are always asking me to watch out for you and yet the number of times I've gone off and left you to get home on your own or asked one of the girls to make sure you get home . . .'

'I know. It could happen so easily. Dad lost his sister. He couldn't prevent that, but he needn't have lost his best friend.'

A moment later, Luke came in to join us and Tony went to get him a drink from the counter. Luke sat in the chair next to me and took my hand. I was about to tell him that I hadn't had a chance to speak to Dad yet, when a familiar car drove past and slowed down for the lights at the pelican crossing. It was a black BMW. Our car. And

Dad was in the driving seat. He glanced in the window at Costa and his face lit up when he saw me. He waved, then he saw Luke next to me and his face clouded. He pulled over at the kerb, much to the annoyance of whoever was behind him, and beckoned for me to come out of the café.

'Dad's out there,' I said to Luke. 'Won't be a moment. Maybe he'll come and join us.'

Outside, Dad waved at me to get into the car, so I slid into the passenger seat and gave him a big hug.

'Hi, Dad.'

'I thought I asked you not to see that boy,' he said.

'It's OK,' I said. 'I know everything.'

'What do you mean, you know everything?'

'Luke's mum told me the whole story. About Nadia . . .'

Dad looked like he was going to explode. 'She *what*? She had no right doing that. It's not her business.'

'I saw photos, Dad. In her album. She didn't know who I was. There was a picture of you and Luke's dad and Aunt Nadia. Luke asked who the girl in the photo was.'

Dad took a couple of very deep breaths as though trying to calm himself.

'It wasn't Mrs De Biasi's fault it all came out, but it did,' I blustered. 'And then I watched *Saving Private Ryan* and it made me realise that life is too short to have any kind of war, big or little and . . . and then I watched *It's a*

Wonderful Life and I realised that your friends and family are the most important thing . . .'

But Dad didn't seem to be listening. He was staring ahead with a grim look on his face.

'Come and meet Luke again,' I said. 'He's in there with Tony.'

'With Tony?'

I nodded.

'You tell him to come out at once. I don't want you mixing with that family.'

'Why not, Dad? You're being totally unreasonable. What happened was a long time ago. It's all in the past . . . And it wasn't Gianni, I mean Mr De Biasi's fault Nadia died. He almost died himself. You must see that. It might have been you in that car with her and she would have still died. You just feel guilty about it. It's mad. It was the fault of the drunk driver who drove into them. No one else's fault.'

'We'll continue this discussion at home,' said Dad and he started up the engine. I quickly got out of the car. Dad leaned over and wound down the window. 'Nesta. Back in the car. Now.'

'No. I'm going back into Costa, then I'm going to the De Biasis' restaurant and I'm not coming home until you come and talk to Luke's dad.'

'Nesta, get in the car.'

I turned my back and walked towards Costa, where I

could see Luke and Tony looking out of the window with concern. Behind them, I caught a glimpse of TJ, Izzie and Lucy in the queue at the counter. They must have arrived while I was in the car with Dad. It wasn't meant to be like that, I thought as I went back in to join them. It was meant to be one of the best moments of Dad's life. I'd wanted to make him really happy after all he'd been through, but instead I'd never seen him look so mad. Or sad.

'Well that went well,' I said as I rejoined Tony and Luke.

'You OK?' asked Luke.

'Yeah, course,' I said, then sighed. 'Parents, huh? You try your best to keep them on the right track, but sometimes they won't listen . . .' I tried my best to smile and make light of what had just happened, but instead, I burst into tears.

Big Realisation

People don't always want what you want for them.

Chapter 15

Stand Off

'I'd never dare defy my dad like that,' said TJ as we made our way down Jackson's Lane on the way to Biasi's. 'He'd throw me out or something.'

'Dad would never do that,' I said, 'but he did look upset.' Privately I was wondering if I had pushed my luck a bit too far. I didn't know what had come over me as I'm not usually that disobedient, but then Dad and I don't usually argue.

'I think you should go home,' said TJ. 'Give him time to adjust to the idea that the whole story about your aunt is out. It's a biggie for him. He must have felt he let everyone down at the time and now you know about it. He probably wants to be the hero in your eyes. You need to tell him he still is and that everyone makes mistakes and has regrets.'

'I did, sort of. I told him that the only person responsible for Nadia's death was the drunk driver. But he wasn't listening. What do you think I should do, Lucy?'

'God, I don't know. Go home and give him a hug. I feel really sorry for him.'

I felt such a failure. Giving Dad a big hug is exactly what I'd meant to do. Part of my fantasy of organising the great reunion. Hah. So much for my mediator, peace-making, healing-the-past skills. Me and my big mouth. Nothing ever comes out right.

Luke and Tony had walked ahead of the rest of us. They seemed to get on really well and I couldn't help but think that Dad and Luke's dad must have looked just like them when they were younger. I was really chuffed that Tony had decided to come with me and support me. He didn't always take my side, but I think he wanted to get this sorted. Or it may be because he thinks that, if Dad doesn't come round, then he'll never let him drive. On the other hand, it may be because Lucy is coming with us and it's a chance for him to hang out with her a bit more. At that moment, he turned and caught Lucy's eye and they smiled at each other. Yeah, he's definitely come along because of Lucy.

As we walked on, I considered my options. Should I go home and give Dad a hug and say I was sorry? Should I let the reunion with Mr De Biaisi go and not push him? Then I remembered the Frank Capra film last night. The whole story seemed to be saying that things happen for a reason. We meet the people that we meet in life for a purpose. Of all the families, in all of London, I meet the De Biasis. It *had* to be fate. I decided to ask the destiny expert.

'What do you think I should do, Iz?'

'Hmmmm,' said Izzie. 'I think you should . . . I dunno, er . . . be prepared to be flexible. Prepared to bend. Yeah, that's it. I read in one of my books that you have to be like a branch on a tree. You know, it bends in the wind. Whereas stuff that doesn't bend or resists, gets broken.'

'Right,' I said, feeling none the wiser. Sometimes I don't quite get Izzie's advice. 'Yeah. OK. I'll be a branch on a tree. You got any last bits of wisdom to pass on, TJ?'

'Don't ask me,' she said. 'You have to decide.'

'Well I'm going to Biasi's,' I said, 'and I'm going to stick to my guns and not budge until Dad comes to talk to them.'

'Then I hope you like pasta,' said Lucy.

'Why?'

'Because you might be there for a very long time.'

Ten minutes later, we all trooped into Biasi's. It was still early and there weren't any customers for lunch yet, so Luke took advantage of the quiet time to do introductions, then fill his mum and dad in on the latest. Seeing their reaction, my reunion fantasy faded even more. They were horrified.

'Oh *no*. Oh Nesta, I'm so sorry,' said Mrs De Biasi. 'I remember how stubborn your dad could be. When he'd made his mind up about something, there was no shifting him.'

Tony laughed. 'One of the many traits he's passed down to his daughter. They're both as stubborn as mules, so this stand-off will be interesting. See who backs down first.'

'Well, it won't be me,' I said.

'No please, Nesta, go home,' said Mrs De Biasi. 'We don't want to come between you and your family. It's the last thing we want.'

'I can't. Not now.'

Mr De Biasi came over and stood in front of me. 'Nesta, go home,' he urged. 'Your father blames me for enough as it is. I don't need this on top. It will only stir everything up again. If he doesn't want to see us, then we must respect that.'

Lucy put her hand on my arm. 'He's right,' she said. 'This might hinder rather than help. Remember what Mum said about not pushing people before they were ready.'

Tony nodded. 'Yeah. Best leave it, sis. It's Dad's call, not yours.'

I was just starting to think that maybe they were right when I saw our car draw up outside the restaurant. Dad was driving and Mum was in the passenger seat. 'Ohmigod! They're here,' I gasped.

I saw Dad glance in at the window, then quickly look away. It must have been quite a shock for him seeing all of us staring back out at him.

'Come away from the door,' said Mrs De Biasi bustling everyone to sit at a table. 'Don't stare at him.'

Two minutes later, the door opened and Mum came in.

I quickly introduced her to Luke's mum and dad and she was very sweet to them, although she gave me a 'Just wait till I get you home, madam' look. 'I'm so sorry about all this family stuff,' she said to the De Biasis, 'You seem to have got caught up in the middle.'

'No, please, we were so happy to hear that Matteo is well,' said Mr De Biasi, 'and to meet Nesta . . .'

'She's so like her father,' said Mrs De Biasi, glancing out of the window with a wistful look.

'Well, I've come to take her home,' said Mum. 'It's lunch-time and Matt wants to spend some time with her and Tony before he has to go back off to Bristol.'

I wasn't fooled. 'So why did Dad come here with you? You could have come on your own.'

Mum sighed. 'Don't be difficult, Nesta. He offered to give me a lift.'

'I think he wants to see the De Biasis more than he's letting on,' I said. 'He needn't have driven you to come and get me. He doesn't usually. It's the unconscious mind thingee, oh you explain Izzie, you know, where your subconscious makes you do what your conscious mind won't let you.'

Suddenly Mr De Biasi got up. 'Enough,' he said and he walked out and got straight into the car with Dad.

'Ohmigod, ohmigod,' I said and dashed to the window to try and see what was going on. I could see that they were in the car and were talking, Mr De Biasi gesticulating and Dad staring ahead. Everything that Jo had told us about body language on the acting class was so evident. I couldn't hear what was being said, but it was clear that Dad was closed off and Mr De Biasi was trying to reach him.

It was Mum who called me away. 'Let them have their privacy,' she said.

'But Mum, this is the big moment . . .' I started.

'Your mother's right,' said Mrs De Biasi. 'Let them be.'

It was agony having to tear myself away from the window. If I'd had my way, I'd have gone and sat in the back seat and stuck my head in between them, so that I could have heard *exactly* what was being said and witnessed every facial expression and *every* shift of body language. But no, Mum made me sit with my back to the window and sip Diet Coke. My mum and Luke's made an effort to get on despite the strange circumstances and everyone else was chatting and laughing and having a good time, but for me the next fifteen minutes seemed to go on forever. It seemed like the dads had been out there for hours.

After what seemed like an eternity, I got up.

'Nesta,' warned Mum. 'Leave them.'

'Yeah. Will,' I said. 'Just going to the ladies.'

As I got up to go to the cloakrooms, I turned and had a quick peak out of the window. They were getting out of the car. Ohmigod, I thought, I hope it's OK and they're not going to fight or anything embarrassing like that. But no, Dad seemed to be dabbing his eyes and . . . yes . . . now he was smiling.

'Nesta,' said Mum, 'I *said* to leave them.'

'But . . . but they've got out of the car,' I said. 'Something's happening.'

Now even Mum couldn't resist looking. She stood up and peeked out, then everyone else did as well. Mr De Biasi was saying something to Dad and Dad creased up laughing. Then the two of them started walking towards the restaurant. For a brief second, I saw the boys that they were, Luke and Tony grown older. The moment after that was hysterical, as everyone dived for their places and tried to look nonchalant, like they hadn't really been gawping outside watching the dads' every move.

The door opened and they came in. Dad was still laughing as he turned to look at me. 'Gianni has just been telling me that you thought Luke was my long lost son . . .'

'Der . . . um, wah . . .' I started, then turned to Mr De Biasi. 'But how did you know?'

Mr De Biasi glanced at Luke, who looked sheepish for a moment. 'Well, I had to check out that it wasn't true, so I asked Mum,' he said, 'and she told Dad.'

Mrs De Biasi had been standing there silently beaming and suddenly she couldn't contain herself any more. 'Ciao, Matteo,' she said, rushing forward with open arms.

Dad turned to her and beamed back. 'Catarina,' he said, then he was enveloped in a huge hug.

Then Mr De Biasi couldn't hold back either and he and Dad looked at each other and gave each other a huge bear hug.

At last, it was the Kodak moment, but of course no one had a camera. Mum's eyes had misted over. Mrs and Mr De Biasi both had their arms around Dad. Tony, Luke, Lucy, Izzie and TJ were grinning like idiots. It was fab.

Chapter 16

Roses and Garlic

'I think friendship is the most important thing in life,' I said as I smeared aloe vera gel over my chin. It was a couple of weeks after le grando reunioni and Lucy, TJ, Izzie and I were lined up on the bathtub doing our Sunday morning monthly beauty routine. This time, I'd been down to the chemists and bought four gel face packs. Proper ones that didn't dribble down your neck or have raw egg in them. *Au naturel* dribbly gloops may be homemade and healthy, but they really aren't my style.

'So do I,' said Lucy. 'We must all make a pact that nothing will ever come between us, like it did for Nesta's and Luke's dads. They wasted years.'

'Each of them had their families,' said TJ, 'so it wasn't totally wasted time.'

'Yeah, but there's that saying, you can't pick your family, but you can pick your friends,' said Izzie. 'Friends are like a chosen family.'

'But whether it's friends or family, you have to keep talking,' I said. 'Say how you feel, even if it's a bit confrontational.'

Seems I started a craze with the De Biasi thing. Confrontation. Tony confronted Dad about driving lessons and, although he hasn't exactly said yes, he didn't say no either, so there's hope. Luke confronted his dad about wanting to be an actor and his dad said he'd think about it. Again, it's a start. And Mum confronted her bosses at work about cutting her hours and they said they'd do what they could to give her more time and reassured her that she had a secure job with them no matter how many younger faces they brought in. And I wasn't left out of the loop. Dad had a go at me about butting into other people's business. 'You don't always know what's best for everyone all the time, Nesta,' he said. 'Yes, I'm glad to see Gianni again, but I would have preferred to have done it in my own time.' I did apologise, but privately I think it's a good job that I pushed him. I know what 'in his own time' means from having him as a dad all these years. It's like when Mum asks him to mend a door or change a light bulb. He says he will, 'in his own time', which means never. He probably even means to, but Mum has learned that if she wants something doing, it's often quicker to do it herself.

So, all in all, there's been a lot going on, but I think it's all been for the best. Our family is certainly talking about stuff more openly than we did before. On top of all the confrontation and communication, the girls and I have decided that we have to have lots of jobs when we grow up, so that all our eggs aren't in one basket career-wise. Tony said he thought I ought to be a journalist as well as an actress and when I asked him why, he said because I speak in headlines. Huh! I don't know *what* he means.

Dad never did tell us what he and Mr De Biasi said in the car, but whatever it was, it mended the rift between them and we've been invited for Sunday lunch with them. We're also having a big birthday bash there as a late celebration for Tony's eighteenth. I get the feeling that the De Biasis are going to be regulars in our lives from now on. Hhhm. Don't know how I feel about that. My parents being chummy with my boyfriend's parents. Is it a good idea? Tony's removed himself from the cosy set-up already. He's taking Lucy out next weekend, but he's taking her to some place in Hampstead. 'Somewhere where no one knows us, so no one will be watching us and seeing what we're getting up to.' Hhmm, I thought, sounds like he has something in mind. I'd better warn Lucy, but on second thoughts, she can handle herself these days.

* * *

After we'd rinsed off our face packs, we got down to the serious business of painting our nails. Izzie pulled out a bottle of her favourite colour and a pack of stick-on diamonds.

'Want any of these?' she asked.

Looking at them gave me a brilliant idea.

'Yes please,' I said and took the sheet she was holding out to me.

I went to the mirror and stuck the diamonds on my brace, then I turned and smiled. 'Designer braces. What do you think?'

Izzie and TJ cracked up. 'Excellent,' said TJ. 'A million dollar smile.'

'Yeah,' I said. 'I decided I can't go round for the next year hiding behind my hand. I decided I'm going to wear my brace with pride.'

'Does it still hurt having it in?' asked TJ.

'No. It hasn't hurt for ages,' I said. 'It's like it's hardly there now.'

Lucy came back in with a tray of Cokes, so I smiled for her too. 'Cool. Mouth jewellery,' she said as she handed me a Coke. 'You'll start a trend.'

'I've also been thinking,' I said. 'All that stuff about being shallow, well, I've decided that it's not a bad thing and, actually, I like being the way I am. So,' I raised my Coke, 'here's a toast to frivolity.'

'What's brought this on?' asked TJ.

'I've been thinking about it a lot over the last few weeks. I was really worried that you all thought I was lightweight, you know, shallow, but I realised something the other night when I was at Luke's house watching his war film. I'll never be into heavy stuff like politics or war. I'll never be into reading literary-type books with clever words that only brainboxes understand. But I've realised that it doesn't matter. There's room for everyone and that includes people who are lightweight, in fact there are times people *want* lightweight. There's room for all types of films, for all types of books and for all types of people. And one sort shouldn't make the other sort feel unworthy or inferior. This is my new philosophy. There's a place for black and there's a place for pink. Room for garlic *and* for roses. Garlic smells um . . . garlicky, roses smell sweet. There's a time and place for both of them, but imagine if the rose suddenly developed a complex because it smelled flowery and not pungent. It would be really sad. No. As I said, everything has its place. Same with people. We're all different and that's what makes life interesting. You can't *be* everything and *know* about everything nor can you be what you're not. Shouldn't even try to be. Um, a rose shouldn't try to be garlic, nor the other way round. Um . . . what am I trying to say? Um . . . that all you can be is true to yourself.'

Izzie was giving me a really strange look, then she cracked up laughing.

'What? I asked. '*What?*"

'Just . . . wow,' said Izzie. 'That's *really* deep.'

'Is it?'

'Yeah,' said TJ. 'And it's exactly what Shakespeare wrote in *Hamlet*. "To thine own self be true, And it must follow, as the night the day, Thou canst not then be false to any man."'

'Really? Then he sounds really cool, does old Shakespearie dearie,' I said, feeling really chuffed that Izzie had said I was deep. 'Yeah. Yo! Shakespeare. My man.'

'To thine own self be true,
And it must follow, as the night the day,
Thou canst not then be false to any man.'
From *Hamlet,* by Shakespeare

'Be true to yourself. (Unless your roots need doing.)'
Nesta Williams (deep person)

Also available by Cathy Hopkins

The MATES, DATES series

1. Mates, Dates and Inflatable Bras
2. Mates, Dates and Cosmic Kisses
3. Mates, Dates and Portobello Princesses
4. Mates, Dates and Sleepover Secrets
5. Mates, Dates and Sole Survivors
6. Mates, Dates and Mad Mistakes
7. Mates, Dates and Pulling Power
8. Mates, Dates and Tempting Trouble
9. Mates, Dates and Great Escapes
10. Mates, Dates and Chocolate Cheats
11. Mates, Dates and Diamond Destiny
12. Mates, Dates and Sizzling Summers

Companion Books:

Mates, Dates Guide to Life

Mates, Dates and You

Mates, Dates Journal

The TRUTH, DARE, KISS OR PROMISE series

1. White Lies and Barefaced Truths
2. Pop Princess
3. Teen Queens and Has-Beens
4. Starstruck
5. Double Dare
6. Midsummer Meltdown
7. Love Lottery
8. All Mates Together

The CINNAMON GIRL series

1. This Way to Paradise
2. Starting Over

Find out more at www.piccadillypress.co.uk
Join Cathy's Club at www.cathyhopkins.com